Rainbow Magic

Special Edition

COLLECTION

Rainbow Magic

Special Edition

COLLECTION

Belle the Birthday Fairy

Florence the Friendship Fairy

Chelsea the Congratulations Fairy

by Daisy Meadows

SCHOLASTIC INC.

If you purchased this book without a cover, you should be aware
that this book is stolen property. It was reported as
"unsold and destroyed" to the publisher, and neither the author
nor the publisher has received any payment for this "stripped book."

Text and illustrations pages 1–169 copyright © 2010 by Rainbow Magic Limited
Text and illustrations pages 170-335 copyright © 2011 by Rainbow Magic Limited
Text and illustrations pages 336-500 copyright © 2015 by Rainbow Magic Limited

All rights reserved. Published by Scholastic Inc., *Publishers since 1920*. SCHOLASTIC
and associated logos are trademarks and/or registered trademarks of Scholastic
Inc. RAINBOW MAGIC is a trademark of Rainbow Magic Limited. Reg. U.S. Patent
& Trademark Office and other countries. HIT and the HIT logo are trademarks
of HIT Entertainment Limited.

The publisher does not have any control over and does not assume any
responsibility for author or third-party websites or their content.

No part of this publication may be reproduced, stored in a retrieval system, or
transmitted in any form or by any means, electronic, mechanical, photocopying,
recording, or otherwise, without written permission of the publisher. For
information regarding permission, write to Scholastic Inc., Attention:
Permissions Department, 557 Broadway, New York, NY 10012.

This book is a work of fiction. Names, characters, places, and incidents are
either the product of the author's imagination or are used fictitiously, and any
resemblance to actual persons, living or dead, business establishments, events,
or locales is entirely coincidental.

ISBN 978-1-338-10243-7

10 9 8 7 6 5 4 3 2 1   16 17 18 19 20

Printed in the U.S.A.   40
First printing 2016

This magical collection includes the
following three special editions!

Contents

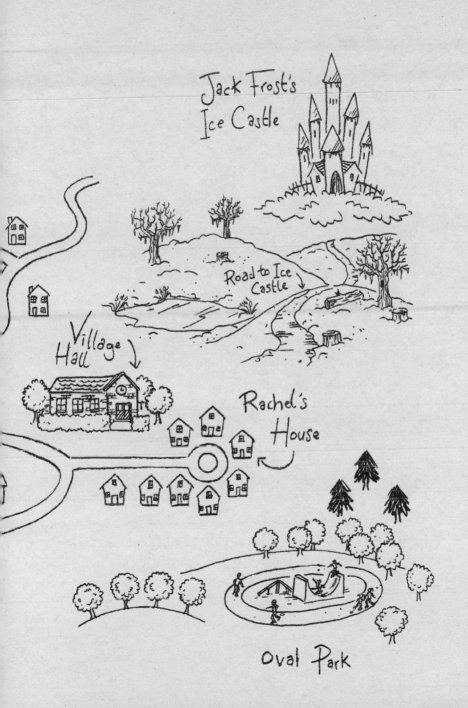

Birthdays come to everyone,
But getting older's not much fun!
Make birthday boys and girls feel bad—
Make them miserable and sad!

Banish presents, cakes, and candles!
Turn their parties into scandals.
This year's birthday treat will be:
All birthdays filled with misery!

**Find the hidden letters in the presents
throughout this book. Unscramble all 5 letters
to spell a special birthday word!**

The Birthday Book

Contents

Parties in Peril!

"I can't wait to see Mom's face when she arrives at her surprise birthday party!" Rachel Walker said with a little skip of excitement.

"Yes, she'll be so amazed when she realizes that you and your dad arranged it all!" replied her best friend, Kirsty Tate, swinging her rollerskates happily.

Kirsty was staying at Rachel's house in Tippington during school break. Rachel's mom thought that Kirsty was just there for a visit, but she was also there to attend Mrs. Walker's surprise party!

"Everything's ready," said Rachel, counting things off on her fingers. "The food, the music, the decorations for the village hall . . ."

"What about the cake?" Kirsty asked.

"Dad ordered that from the bakery," said Rachel with a smile. "He's not very good at baking, and he wanted it to be perfect!"

The friends were on their way to the local park to go rollerskating. As they passed the village hall where Mrs.

Walker's party was going to be, Rachel
squeezed Kirsty's hand.

"Let's just quickly look inside," she said.
"I want to show you where I'm planning
to put all the decorations on the day of
the party."

"Ooh, yes!" said Kirsty eagerly. "I can't
wait to help you decorate the hall and
lay out the food."

They peeked in the door—and their

mouths fell open in astonishment. A group
of boys and girls were there in their best
party outfits, but no one seemed to be
having a good time. The guests were
talking in low voices. They all looked
upset! Some of the parents were kneeling
on the floor, cleaning up squished cakes
and spilled drinks. A box of decorations
sat untouched by the window. There was
a stereo on the stage, but it was making

a strange whining sound and there was
smoke coming out of the top.

A little girl was standing by the door
with her head down. She was wearing a
pretty pink dress with a white sash, but
she looked very sad.

"Hello," said Rachel. "Is this your
party?"

The little girl nodded her head. Her big
blue eyes filled with tears.

"Everything's going wrong!" she sobbed. "Half of the guests forgot my birthday party and didn't show up. The food tables collapsed and squished my birthday cake. None of the decorations would stay up on the walls. Now the stereo is broken, so we can't even dance." Kirsty put her arm around the little girl's shaking shoulders. She didn't know what to say.

The girl's mom hurried over to them.

"I'm sorry, Maya, but Dad can't fix the stereo. We're going to have to move the party home."

"But we can't fit everyone in our house," said Maya, looking miserable.

"I know, but we have no choice," said her mom sadly. "You can pick ten friends to bring with you. Everyone else will just have to go home."

Trying not to cry again, Maya walked off with her mom. Rachel and Kirsty left and headed toward the park.

"I feel so bad for Maya," said Rachel. "It's really unlucky that all those things went wrong."

When they got to the park, they sat down to put on their rollerskates. They were both upset about the little

girl's birthday being ruined!

"If only one of the Party Fairies had been here," Kirsty said with a sigh. "I'm sure they could have done something."

Rachel and Kirsty were good friends with the fairies, and had often helped them outwit mean Jack Frost and his mischievous goblins.

The girls stood up, wobbled a little, and held onto each other for balance. For a

moment, they forgot about the ruined party.

"It's been ages since you and I went rollerskating!" Rachel giggled. "I hope I can still remember how to skate without falling over!"

A New Fairy Friend

Rachel and Kirsty had only been rollerskating for a few minutes when a group of older boys walked by carrying skateboards. They all looked annoyed. Rachel spotted a boy who lived on her street in the group.

"Hi, Sam!" she called. "Have you guys been skateboarding on the park ramp?"

"Only for about five minutes," said Sam. "It's Oliver's birthday, so we were planning a whole day of skateboarding. But the ramp collapsed and the park worker sent us home. It's the only ramp in Tippington, so Oliver's birthday plans are ruined."

"That's so unlucky!" said Rachel. "Two birthdays ruined in one day!"

Kirsty frowned as the boys walked away.

"It's more than unlucky," she said. "It's too much of a coincidence."

"You're right, Kirsty!" said a musical voice behind them.

The girls whirled around in surprise.
The tall hedge behind them was
sparkling with colored lights. Sitting
cross-legged on one of the leaves was
a tiny fairy! She had long brown hair
pulled back on one side with a purple
flower. She was wearing a pretty purple
minidress with sparkly gold ballet flats.

"Hi, girls," she said with a friendly smile. "I'm Belle the Birthday Fairy!"

"Hi, Belle!" said Rachel and Kirsty, stepping closer to the hedge so that other people wouldn't be able to see the little fairy.

"Is everything OK?" Kirsty asked. "We've seen two birthdays go wrong already this morning."

Belle's smile faded and she nodded sadly.

"King Oberon and Queen Titania sent me to ask for your help," she said anxiously. "There's no time to lose. Jack Frost has stolen the magic birthday charms!"

"What are the birthday charms?" Rachel asked in alarm.

"The birthday charms make sure that birthdays go smoothly in Fairyland and the human world," Belle explained. "Now that Jack Frost has hidden them somewhere, birthdays everywhere are going horribly wrong!"

Rachel's hand flew to her mouth.

"Oh, no!" she cried. "That means Mom's special surprise party on Saturday could be ruined!"

"Can you help me?" asked Belle. "Will you come with me to Fairyland and search for clues that might lead us to the birthday charms?"

"Of course!" cried Rachel and Kirsty together.

Belle fluttered above them and waved her wand. A burst of purple and gold fairy dust swirled out of the wand's tip and showered down on the girls. They felt themselves shrinking to the same size as Belle. Beautiful wings appeared on their backs, and Rachel and Kirsty fluttered them in delight. It was a wonderful feeling!

Belle waved her wand again. This time, the multicolored sparkles spun around them in a dizzying circle.

"It's like a merry-go-round!" Kirsty

gasped, tightly squeezing her best friend's
hand.

A few moments later, the colorful blur
faded away — and the girls were flying
over Fairyland!

Goblin Intruders

"I thought we could start by flying over Fairyland and looking for clues," said Belle.

"So, what are the birthday charms?" asked Kirsty, as they fluttered above the emerald-green hills and tiny toadstool houses. "What exactly are we looking for?"

"There are three magic birthday charms," said Belle. "There's the birthday book, the birthday candle, and the birthday present. The birthday book lists the birthdays of everyone in both the human world and Fairyland. Without it, nobody knows when *anyone's* birthday is!"

"No wonder half of Maya's guests didn't show up today," said Rachel thoughtfully.

"The birthday candle makes all birthday cakes delicious and grants birthday wishes," Belle went on. "And the birthday present makes sure that everyone receives the perfect birthday gift."

"Oh my goodness!" said Kirsty. "Without those charms, nobody will ever have a happy birthday again!"

"I think that's why Jack Frost stole them," Belle said, nodding. "You see, it's his birthday soon, and he's feeling really miserable about his age."

"So he wants everyone else to be miserable, too?" Rachel guessed. "How mean!"

"He doesn't want anyone to find out when his birthday is—not even the goblins," said Belle. "But without the magic birthday book, we won't know when *anyone's* birthday is!"

The three fairies flew along, scanning the land below. They were directly over the glittering towers of the magical Fairyland Palace when Kirsty gave a cry and pointed down.

"Look!" she exclaimed.

Far below, they could see three goblins scrambling up a ladder and climbing over the back wall of the palace!

"I'm sure they're up to no good!" said Belle. "Come on. Let's find out what's happening!"

Rachel, Kirsty, and Belle zoomed after the goblins as they crept through a back door of the palace. The fairies followed, turning a corner to see the goblins tiptoeing into the Palace Library.

"I'm going to give those goblins a piece of my mind!" exclaimed Belle. "How dare they sneak into the palace?"

She surged forward, her cheeks pink

with indignation. Kirsty grabbed her arm and stopped her.

"Wait!" she whispered. "What if this has something to do with the birthday charms? Let's creep in and listen to what they're saying—it might give us a clue." Belle nodded, so the three fairies slipped silently into the warm, cozy library. The high walls were lined with books, some of them sparkling with magic. In the middle of the room were six squishy armchairs. Beside each armchair was a round wooden table with

a glowing lamp on top of it.

"I don't think the goblins are here
to read quietly," whispered Rachel
as they ducked behind an armchair.
"Look!"

The goblins were pulling books off the shelves, row after row, and throwing them on the floor.

"Did you find it?" hissed the tallest goblin to the others.

"Not yet!" they replied.

"Well, hurry up!" the tall goblin told them. "If we can't find the birthday

book, we won't know when Jack Frost's birthday is — and we won't be able to plan his surprise party!"

Rachel, Kirsty, and Belle stared at each other in amazement. The magic birthday

book was hidden here in the Palace
Library!

"It sounds like the goblins want to find
the birthday book as much as we do,"
Kirsty whispered. "Let's try and convince
them to help us!"

Belle looked doubtful.

"The goblins are never very helpful,"
she said.

"I think it's worth a try," said Rachel.
"After all, they're disobeying Jack Frost
by being here," she pointed out. "He
doesn't want them to find the birthday
book, so they must have a good reason
for ignoring his orders. I think we should
try to find out what it is!"

"Besides, it might take the three of us
a long time to find the birthday book
ourselves," Kirsty agreed, looking at all

the books that lined the walls. "We could use the goblins' help searching for it."

Belle agreed, so they stepped out from behind the armchair and walked toward the goblins, who were still busily throwing books onto the floor. The girls tiptoed up behind them as quictly as they could. . . .

Birthday Book Hunt

"It was a good idea for Jack Frost to hide the birthday book here, wasn't it?" said Rachel in a loud voice.

The goblins spun around in surprise.

"We would never have thought of looking here if it hadn't been for you goblins," Belle agreed. "We should thank you!"

"Jack Frost knew that you silly fairies would never think to look under your

own noses!" said the smallest goblin, sticking out his tongue. "Leave us alone!"

"Don't be so rude!" said Belle. "We want to help you."

"No way!" squeaked the goblins together.

"Listen to me, goblins," said Kirsty in a friendly voice. "We overheard what you said about throwing a surprise party for Jack Frost. You need that book as much as we do. How about making a deal with us?"

"What sort of deal?" asked the tallest goblin suspiciously.

"You snuck into the palace, and that's not allowed," said Kirsty. "We should really tell you to leave right away. So here's the deal," she continued. "We'll let you stay and look up Jack Frost's birthday in the birthday book, if you promise to return the book to Belle when you're done."

The goblins gathered into a little

huddle. The girls could hear them arguing in loud whispers. But after a few minutes, they turned around and nodded.

"It's a deal!" they said in unison. Then the great birthday book hunt began! The goblins had no idea where in the library Jack Frost had hidden the book. The goblins searched the lower shelves, and the girls flew up to search the shelves that the goblins couldn't reach.

The hunt went on and on. Rachel's arms were aching from pulling out each heavy book to check it, and Kirsty's wings were getting tired from hovering in one position for so long. Belle kept flitting down to the lower shelves to clean up the books that the goblins were throwing onto the floor.

Outside the tall library windows, the sun began to set. It was getting late, and they still hadn't found the magic birthday book!

"Are you absolutely sure that he hid it in here?" Kirsty asked as she reached the end of another row of books.

"Positive," said the middle goblin, wiping a few beads of sweat off his brow. "He said, 'Those pesky fairies will never guess that I've hidden the book in the Palace Library. I hope it makes them feel really uncomfortable!'"

"That's a strange thing to say," said Kirsty, fluttering to the ground to give her wings a rest.

Rachel flew down to join her. "Maybe we're looking in the wrong place," she said thoughtfully. "After all, Jack Frost didn't say that he had hidden the book on the shelves. He said that he wanted to make the fairies *uncomfortable*."

They all thought hard for a moment, and then Kirsty's eyes began to sparkle.

"What if that's exactly what he

meant?" she said. "What if it's in one of the armchairs?"

Everyone stared at each other for a minute, and then each of them rushed to one of the six armchairs. They pulled up the seat cushions and the smallest goblin gave a yell of triumph.

"I've got it!"

Discoveries!

The little goblin waved a shining book above his head, but he didn't have a very good grip on it. The book flew through the air and landed safely in Belle's arms.

"The birthday book!" she cried in delight.

Rachel, Kirsty, and the three goblins eagerly gathered around Belle. The

birthday book was bound in gold, and
when Belle opened it a puff of colorful
fairy dust covered them all in sparkles.

"Look up Jack Frost's birthday!"
cried the tallest goblin. "You
promised!"

"A fairy always keeps
her promises," said Belle
calmly.

She turned the
shimmering pages
of the book. Hundreds
of thousands of names
were written there in
tiny golden letters!

"There's my mom!"
cried Rachel, pointing out
Mrs. Walker's name as the
page turned.

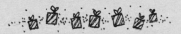

"There's Jack Frost!" exclaimed the goblins all at the same time.

"Oh my goodness!" said Rachel, her eyes opening wide. "Mom's birthday is on exactly the same day as Jack Frost's!" The goblins were delighted to have gotten the information they came for. They ran home as fast as they could, promising that they would never sneak into the palace uninvited ever again.

Belle hugged the birthday book to her chest and gave the girls a big smile.

"I can't thank you enough for helping

me find this!" she
said. "If it
hadn't been
for you I
would have
thrown those
three goblins
out of the
palace. Then
I never would have
found out why they were here."

"I'm so glad we could help," said Kirsty
warmly. "Does this mean that birthdays
go back to normal now?"

"I'm afraid not," said Belle, her smile
fading. "People will remember the dates
of birthdays, but without the magic
birthday candle and birthday present,

things will keep going wrong."

"Then we'll just have to make sure that we find the other two birthday charms soon," said Rachel in a determined voice. "I'm not going to let Jack Frost ruin birthdays for everyone. I'm *definitely* not going to let him ruin my mom's surprise party!"

"I agree," said Kirsty. "Let's get started right away!"

But Belle shook her head.

"I have to return the birthday book to the present-wrapping room now. That's where it's normally kept," she said.

"Besides, look outside!"

Kirsty and Rachel turned
to the library
window. In all
the excitement,
they hadn't
noticed that
night had fallen
in Fairyland. They
could see the stars twinkling and the
moon glowing.

"It's almost my bedtime!" said Belle,
stifling a yawn. "And it's time for you two
to return to the human world."

"Will we see you again soon, so we can
search for the other birthday charms?"
Kirsty asked.

"Of course," said Belle with a smile.
"Good-bye, girls—for now!"

She flicked her wand, and there was
a whoosh of colorful sparkles. The girls
both closed their eyes.

When Kirsty and Rachel opened their
eyes again, they were standing next to
the hedge in the park, and the sun was

shining. In the distance they could see
Oliver and his friends walking away with
their skateboards under their arms.

"No time has passed at all," said
Rachel with a grin. "Oh, Kirsty, I love
magic!"

"Me, too!" said Kirsty, hugging

her friend. "Come on, let's do some rollerskating. Keep your eyes peeled for clues. Jack Frost could have hidden the other two birthday charms anywhere— and that includes the human world!"

The Birthday Candle

Contents

Cake Catastrophe

"I hope it stops raining in time for Mom's surprise birthday party on Saturday," said Rachel as she and Kirsty hurried along, huddling under an umbrella.

"Me, too," Kirsty agreed. "Birthdays are never as much fun when it's raining."

"I wonder if Jack Frost has anything
to do with this rain," said Rachel.

"I don't think we can blame him,"
Kirsty replied with a little giggle. "It's
probably just bad weather."

"I hope Belle is OK," Rachel went on.
"Time's running out! We have to find her
other two charms before Mom's party."

They had helped Belle the Birthday
Fairy find the magic birthday book
that Jack Frost had stolen, but two of
Belle's birthday charms were still missing.
Without them, birthdays were going
wrong all over Fairyland—and in the
human world, too! Rachel didn't want
anyone's party to be ruined, especially
her mom's.

"Let's try not to worry," said Kirsty,
putting her arm around her best friend's

shoulders. "Queen Titania always says that we should let the magic come to us."

"That's true," Rachel replied, her face brightening. "Ack, Kirsty, watch what you're doing with the umbrella! You just dripped water down my back!"

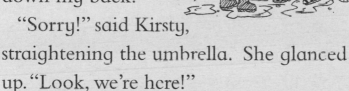

"Sorry!" said Kirsty, straightening the umbrella. She glanced up. "Look, we're here!"

The two girls had arrived at the bakery. Mr. Walker had sent them on a special secret mission to pick up the birthday cake he had ordered for Rachel's mom.

"This window display always makes me

hungry," said Rachel, pausing next to the glass.

"I've never seen so many yummy treats in one place!" Kirsty agreed.

The shelves in the window were filled with a dazzling choice of cakes and pastries. There were pastries covered in fruit, cheesecakes with ruby-red strawberry glaze, and cakes topped with icing and sugared almonds.

The girls leaned closer to read some of the handwritten labels.

Kirsty let out a sigh filled with longing.

"They make the best cakes in Tippington," Rachel told her. "I can't wait to have a piece of the cake they made for Mom."

"Let's go inside and see it!" said Kirsty.

Rachel stepped inside the bakery. Kirsty shook off the umbrella and followed her.

The bakery was full of wonderful smells, and Kirsty felt her stomach start to rumble. The warm scents of cake, chocolate, nuts, and cream filled the air.

"Hello," said Rachel to the plump baker behind the counter. "We've come to pick up the birthday cake for Mrs. Walker." The man's smiling face fell. "Oh, no," he said. "I'm so sorry, but you're going to have to come back tomorrow, instead. I'm having a lot of trouble with that cake."

He pointed to the counter behind him. He had obviously been trying to frost a

cake, but something was very wrong. The
cake was misshapen,
and the icing
was sliding off.
Sugared flowers
were lying
beside it. The baker
looked at them with a
worried expression.

"This is the third cake I've tried to
make for Mrs. Walker," he said. "I've used
the same recipe I use for all birthday
cakes, but it keeps going wrong. The
cake is coming out heavy and dry,
and the icing won't stay put. It's a
nightmare!"

Rachel's eyes filled with tears, but
Kirsty tugged on her arm.

"We'll come back tomorrow," she told the baker. "Come on, Rachel."

"Why did we leave so quickly?" asked Rachel as they stepped outside the shop.

"Because of what I just saw out the window!" Kirsty whispered urgently.

She pointed at three people who were crowding under one small umbrella and gazing at the cake display. Rachel rubbed her eyes and did a double take.

All three of them were wearing rainboots, raincoats, and rain hats. Between the top of the boots and the bottom of the raincoats, she could see green legs.

She gasped. "They're goblins!"

Goblins in Tippington!

Rachel and Kirsty stared in amazement as the three goblins put down their umbrella and scurried into the bakery. They tracked rainwater all over the bakery floor as they splashed inside.

"What are the goblins doing in

Tippington?" Kirsty wondered out loud.

"I don't know," said Rachel, "but *we're* getting soaked! Put the umbrella up, quick!" Kirsty raised the umbrella above their heads, but as she opened it something strange happened. The inside of the umbrella glowed with colored lights—and then Belle spiraled down the handle, waving at them!

"Belle!" exclaimed Kirsty. "Thank

goodness you're here. Three goblins just
went into the bakery!"

"I know," said Belle,
folding her arms.
"I'm sure they're
planning some
trouble. I saw them
creep out of Jack
Frost's Ice Castle at
dawn, and they were
acting suspicious, so I

followed them. I'm glad to find you girls
here. How did you know that the goblins
were coming?"

"We didn't," Rachel explained. "We just
saw them when we came to pick up the
cake for my mom's surprise party."

"Something keeps going wrong with

the cake recipe," Kirsty added. "The
baker can't make it work."

Belle's face fell.

"I knew this would happen," she said
with a sigh. "The magic birthday candle
helps all birthday cakes to bake perfectly
and grants the birthday person a wish.
Until I find it, I'm afraid no birthday
cakes are going to turn out well."

"Belle, could you turn us into fairies?"
asked Kirsty. "We have to find out what
those goblins are up to."

"Good idea!" Belle said. "But I can't do
magic here in the middle of the street."

"Let's go over there," said Rachel,
pointing to a little alleyway between
the bakery and the store next door.

The girls hurried down the alley and
stopped when they were sure that no one

could see them from the street. Then Belle waved her wand. A flurry of gold and purple fairy dust twinkled around the girls. It was like being caught in a storm of sequins! They giggled happily as the fairy dust settled. They had shrunk down to the same size as Belle, and their gauzy wings were glistening in all different colors.

"Let's follow those goblins and find out

what they're planning!" said Belle.

She zipped back up the alley with Rachel and Kirsty fluttering close behind. The bakery door was open, and all three of them slipped in through the crack.

"Let's watch from the top of that display cabinet," said Rachel, pointing to a shelf. "No one will see us up there."

They fluttered up to the highest shelf and sat on the edge. They could see the baker bringing out cake after cake to show the goblins. What were they up to?

"These just aren't good enough!" squawked the tallest goblin.

"What a bunch of garbage!" squeaked the smallest goblin.

They were causing trouble already!

Kitchen Chaos

The baker had brought out all his most elaborate cakes and lined them up in front of the goblins. They weren't birthday cakes, so he hadn't had any trouble making them.

"Boring!" shouted the middle goblin, poking his bony finger into the first cake.

"Boring! Boring! Boring!" the other two yelled, poking their fingers into all the beautiful cakes in front of them.

"But this is my best selection!" cried the poor baker. "Ha!" snorted the tallest goblin. "We're from the Cake Standards Board, and I'm telling you that these are terrible cakes! We'll shut this bakery down unless you start making better ones!"

The baker rubbed his forehead, looking upset.

"The Cake Standards Board?" he repeated. "But I've never heard—"

"We could make better cakes than this

standing on our heads, with our eyes shut!" yelled the middle goblin.

"Get out!" screeched the smallest goblin. "Come back in an hour and you'll see a truly magnificent cake!"

"I guess I *could* take my lunch break now," the baker stammered. "It's been a tough morning. . . ."

"Go! Go! GO!" cried the middle goblin, pressing the baker's umbrella into his hands and shoving him toward the door.

The doorbell jangled as the baker left. The goblins locked the door behind him, snickering.

"Those nasty goblins!" cried Rachel, who had been watching in shock. "How could they be so awful to that nice baker?"

"And *why*?" Kirsty added. "What do they want?"

"Let's find out!" said Belle, fluttering into the air. "Look— they're heading into the kitchen at the back of the store!"

The three girls flew through the colorful curtain that separated the store from the kitchen.

"Oh!" Belle gasped.

Suddenly, they were enveloped in a blinding white cloud!

"What is this?" Kirsty coughed, twirling around and trying to see what had happened.

"It's going in my mouth!" Rachel cried. "It's . . . it's . . . flour!"

"Fly upward!" said Belle, coughing as she breathed in the flour dust. "As fast as you can!"

The three girls zoomed toward the ceiling, and their heads broke out of the floury cloud.

As the flour began to settle, they saw
that the three goblins were running
around the kitchen. They had pulled off
their enormous rain hats and raincoats.
The tallest goblin had a chef's hat
perched on his head, and the smallest was
wearing a striped apron. The middle one
seemed jealous, and kept trying to steal
the others' outfits.

The goblins had knocked over a huge bag of flour, which had caused the cloud. The floor and the counter were smeared with broken eggs, dotted with spilled raisins, and dusted with sugar.

"Oh, no!" Kirsty exclaimed. "They're wrecking the kitchen. By the time the baker gets back, everything will be ruined!"

"We have to stop them," said Rachel with a determined expression on her face.

"Wait a minute," said Belle. "I don't think they're here just to make trouble. Look! I think they're actually trying to make a cake!"

The goblins had opened a cookbook, and were stirring lots of ingredients into a large mixing bowl. "Stop pushing me!" squawked the goblin in the chef's hat. He elbowed the goblin in the apron and broke an egg over his head.

"It's my turn to stir!" wailed the middle goblin.

"Oh, be quiet and go get the candle!" the tallest goblin snapped.

The middle goblin pouted. He stomped over to the pile of rain hats and raincoats, and felt in the pockets. Then he pulled out a beautiful cake candle with a magic flame. It was a shimmering purple color, and glittered in the light.

Belle went pale.

"Girls, that's *it*!" she said quietly. "*That's* my magic birthday candle!"

Trapped!

As Rachel, Kirsty, and Belle stared at the birthday candle in excitement, the other two goblins were still arguing.

"I'm the one with the chef's hat, so I'm in charge!" said the tallest goblin, shaking flour into the mixing bowl.

"Oh, yeah?" snarled the one in the apron. "You can't be in charge — you

don't even know how to read a recipe!"
He jabbed a green finger at the long
cookbook. "That says 'add *sugar*', not 'add
flour', you fool!"

"Who are you calling a fool?" shrieked
the other.

They rolled across the bakery floor,
wrestling, and crashed into the shelves.
A colorful waterfall of cake decorations,
ribbons, cake stands, and candle holders
rained down on them.

As the other goblins tumbled around the floor, the middle goblin continued to follow the recipe. Rachel saw him add a large spoonful of chili powder to the mixture and stir it in.

"That cake is going to taste horrible!" she said to Kirsty. "They haven't even broken the eggs properly—I can see pieces of shell in there."

The goblin started to pour the mixture into a cake pan, but he needed both hands, so he put the candle down on the counter.

"Now's our chance!" Rachel whispered.

"I could fly down and pick up the candle before he notices!"

"It's too dangerous!" Belle whispered. "The candle is right next to him. He'll catch you!"

Rachel gulped. She knew that it was dangerous, but she couldn't stand the thought of her mom's birthday cake being ruined because of Jack Frost and the goblins.

"I've got to try," she said.

CRASH! BANG!

The other goblins were still fighting. At that moment, the middle

92

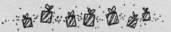

goblin turned to put the cake pan in the
oven. Rachel flew down to the counter as
fast as her wings could flutter, and
Belle and Kirsty both held
their breaths. Could she
grab the candle before
the goblin turned
around again?
Rachel reached the
candle and put her
arms under it, but it
was too heavy!
She couldn't lift herself
and the candle into
the air—and the
goblin was turning around!
Kirsty and Belle darted down to
help Rachel. But before they could
reach her, the goblin gave a yell of alarm.

"It's one of those pesky fairies!"

He grabbed a strainer and brought it crashing upside down on top of Rachel. She was trapped!

The other goblins dashed over to the counter. They were covered in egg, flour, and broken cake decorations, but they grinned when they saw Rachel hammering against the side of the strainer.

"Let me out!" she cried.

"Look, there are more of them!" yelped
the middle goblin, pointing
to where Kirsty and
Belle were
hovering
in the air.

"Aha!" cried
the smallest
goblin, dancing
around and sticking
out his tongue at them. "We caught a
fairy! We caught a fairy!"

Belle put her hands on her hips.

"Goblins, give me the candle and let
Rachel go right now!" she said in a
loud voice.

"No way!" retorted the tallest goblin.

Kirsty frowned. She thought about the

goblins creeping out of Jack Frost's Ice
Castle.

"You're the same goblins who came
looking for the birthday book, aren't
you?" she said, thinking quickly. "Does
Jack Frost know you're here?"

All three goblins went pale green.

"You're not going to tell him, are you?"
asked the smallest goblin in a trembling
voice.

The middle goblin began to sweat. "Oh, no—you can't!"

Kirsty and Belle exchanged confused glances. Why were the goblins causing trouble without orders from Jack Frost?

A Deal is Made

"Don't tell Jack Frost!" said the tallest goblin. "We want it to be a surprise!"

"This cake is for Jack Frost?" Rachel asked.

"Of course!" said the middle goblin. "We couldn't make it in the Ice Castle without him noticing."

"Now go away!" the smallest goblin squeaked.

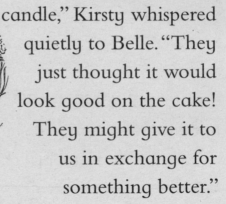

"We're not leaving without Rachel and the birthday candle," Belle declared.

"That's our candle!" snapped the tallest goblin. "We found it next to Jack Frost's throne. Now it's ours, and we're keeping it!"

"They don't know that it's a magic candle," Kirsty whispered quietly to Belle. "They just thought it would look good on the cake! They might give it to us in exchange for something better."

"What are you whispering about?" demanded the tallest goblin.

"We were just talking about the cake you made for Jack Frost's surprise party," Kirsty said. "Without magic, it will take

hours to bake. The baker will be back soon, and he won't be happy with the mess you've made. But if you agree to help us, Belle can make your cake cook faster, and then you can head back to the Ice Castle!"

The goblins made faces at the idea of helping the fairies again. Kirsty couldn't help hoping that their impatience would get the better of them.

"If we agree, we could be back at the castle in time for lunch!" the tallest goblin whispered to the others.

That did it! The greedy goblins nodded in agreement, and Kirsty smiled with relief. Belle waved her wand, and a jet of gold and purple sparkles hit the oven. The door swung open— and the finished cake floated out and landed on the table in front of the goblins! Everyone stared at it open-mouthed.

"It's horrible!" said Kirsty.

"It's spectacular!" the goblins cried.

The cake was gray and formed sharp spikes where pieces of eggshell were sticking out. It was misshapen and ugly . . . but it was *perfect* for Jack Frost.

"It could look even better with icing and decorations," said Kirsty, winking at Belle.

"Yes!" cried the goblins, clapping their hands and dancing around the kitchen in excitement. "Make it better! Make it better!"

"I'll finish the cake for you—in exchange for two things," said Belle. "Let Rachel go, and give me the candle."

"Done!" the middle goblin declared. He lifted the strainer and Rachel flew up to join Kirsty and Belle.

"Thank you, Belle!" She smiled, stretching out her wings. Then Belle flew down to the birthday candle. She picked it up, shrank it to its fairy size, and swept her wand over the cake.

Ribbons of blue and silver fairy dust

began to curl around it. In a sparkle of magic, the cake was transformed into Jack Frost's face, covered with silver-blue

icing and topped with large candles. Belle had even written HAPPY BIRTHDAY in silver balls on the side. "I'll carry it!" shouted the smallest goblin, taking off his apron and lunging for the cake.

"No, *I'll* carry it—you're too clumsy!" yelled the middle goblin, picking up the cake and balancing it above his head.

He raced to the door, closely followed
by the other two goblins, who were still
complaining loudly.

"They didn't even say thank you!" said Kirsty, shaking her head at their rudeness.

"Never mind that," Belle replied, grinning. "I've got the magic birthday candle back!"

"And the baker will be able to make Mom's cake now," added Rachel with a happy smile.

"That poor baker!" Kirsty gasped, staring around at the mess the goblins had made.

"Don't worry!" said Belle, giving them a wink.

She flicked her wand, and the whole room shimmered. When the sparkles faded, the kitchen was gleaming and tidy, and a magnificent cake was sitting on the counter. It was decorated with pink icing

and a border of pink hearts.

"Perfect!" Rachel cried.

Then, with a wave of her wand, Belle
returned Rachel and Kirsty to their
human size.

"I'm taking the magic birthday candle home to Fairyland right away, but I'll see you again soon," she said. "Birthday cakes and wishes are safe—thanks to you two!"

She blew a kiss and disappeared in a flurry of fairy dust. Rachel and Kirsty smiled at each other.

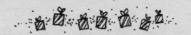

"Now there's only one birthday charm missing," said Rachel. "I just hope that we can find it before Mom's party!"

"I know we can," said Kirsty, sounding confident. "After all, if we can convince those crazy goblins to help us *twice*, we can do anything!"

The Birthday Present

Contents

Party Pooper

"SURPRISE!" everyone shouted.

"Oh my goodness!" exclaimed Mrs. Walker.

Balloons flew into the air, and party poppers cracked all around the village hall, raining colored streamers over the astonished Mrs. Walker. Rachel and Kirsty each took one of her hands and led her into the center of the hall.

"What a wonderful surprise!" Mrs. Walker gasped. "How did you pull this off?"

"I couldn't have done it without these two!" Mr. Walker laughed, putting his arms around Rachel and Kirsty. The guests crowded around Mrs. Walker, hugging her and wishing her a happy birthday.

Rachel and Kirsty smiled at each other. They had spent hours decorating the hall and putting out the food. All the guests had arrived, and then Mrs. Walker had finally walked in. She hadn't suspected a thing!

"Everything's going really well," Kirsty said in a low voice. "I was afraid that Jack Frost would ruin the party because he still has the magic birthday present."

"That reminds me — it's almost time to give Mom her special gift!" said Rachel in excitement. "Dad and I bought her a beautiful jewelry 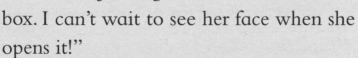 box. I can't wait to see her face when she opens it!"

"Hi, Rachel!" called two girls from

across the room. "Congratulations—
what a great party!"

"Hi, Rosie! Hi, Natalia!" Rachel
replied. "I'm glad you're having fun!"

"The cake looks beautiful!" added a
girl named Emma, whose dad had gone
to school with Mrs. Walker.

"I know—I can't wait to taste it!"
Kirsty said with a grin.

But before it was time for cake, Rachel

and Kirsty helped Mr. Walker carry their large present to Mrs. Walker. Mr. Walker made a little speech, and then everyone sang "Happy Birthday."

"How exciting!" exclaimed Mrs. Walker.

She untied the big purple ribbon and carefully tore the wrapping paper. Rachel hopped from one foot to another. A bubble of excitement rose up inside her as Mrs. Walker opened the box. . . .

"Oh," said Mrs. Walker.

"Oh, no!" groaned Rachel and Kirsty together.

There was no beautiful jewelry box

inside—just a pair of muddy old boots!
Mr. Walker stared at the boots. He seemed to be at a loss for words. "Well . . ." said Mrs. Walker, blinking quickly, "these will be very useful for working in the garden. Thank you!"

But Rachel could see that her mom was upset. Frowning, she tugged on Kirsty's arm and led her away from the other guests.

"It's not fair!" she whispered. "I know that Mom will enjoy her party no matter what presents she gets, but she would have loved that jewelry box!"

Kirsty nodded. "It must be—"

"Are you OK, Rachel?" called her friend Antonia, who had noticed Rachel's worried expression.

"I'm fine, thanks," said Rachel, giving her a smile.

She hurried toward the door and beckoned to Kirsty to follow her. She led the way outside and around to the back of  the hall, where weeds and tall bushes hid them from view.

"*Ouch!*" said Kirsty, as she brushed her

hand against a thistle. "Rachel, where are we going?"

Rachel turned with her hand on the magic locket around her neck. The king and queen of Fairyland had given each of the girls a locket.

They were full of magic fairy dust, which Rachel and Kirsty could use to

take them to Fairyland if they ever
needed help from the fairies.

"We have to help Belle find the magic
birthday present—before anything else
goes wrong at Mom's party!" Rachel
said. "Kirsty, we're off to Fairyland!"

Party
Planners

The girls opened their lockets and sprinkled the fairy dust over their heads. Immediately they were caught up in a swirling cloud of sparkles. The glittering whirl swept them off their feet and carried them through the air.

Rachel and Kirsty felt themselves shrinking to fairy size. Then the sparkles faded away, and the girls were standing outside the glittering silver and pink Fairyland Palace. The large doors were wide open, and the girls could see that the entrance hall was bustling with activity. There were tables full of food, dozens of frog footmen carrying boxes and packages, and dozens of fairies flitting around.

"Oh, Rachel, look!" Kirsty exclaimed in delight. "There's

Joy the Summer Vacation Fairy! And the Rainbow Fairies are over there!"

Just then, they saw Belle hovering in a corner. Rachel and Kirsty waved at her, and she flew quickly over to them.

"Hello, girls!" she said. "I didn't expect to see you here today."

Rachel explained what had happened at her mom's party.

"What a mess!" exclaimed Belle. "Jack Frost has caused so many problems by stealing the magic birthday present. He's even ruined his own surprise party!"

"What do you mean?" Kirsty asked.

"When the king and queen heard that the goblins were planning a surprise birthday party for Jack Frost at the Ice Castle, they offered to help," Belle explained. "But there's a big problem. Follow me!"

She flitted through the palace toward the throne room. The girls followed her, waving to all their fairy friends as they went. The king and queen were sitting on their thrones in the chamber.

Rachel and Kirsty landed before them and curtsied.

"Welcome, girls!" said Queen Titania. "It's wonderful to see you!"

"It's so nice to be here again, Your Majesty," said Rachel breathlessly. "We came because something went wrong at my mom's surprise birthday party. I'm sure it's because Jack Frost still has the magic birthday present."

"I agree," said the queen. "He's very vain, and he didn't want anyone to know that today is his birthday! But we can't prepare anything to take to his birthday party until the final charm is safely back here. That means that the goblins are up at the Ice Castle doing all the work themselves." "Things keep going wrong with the preparations," added King Oberon. "The food is burned and the decorations have gone missing." He sighed. "We have to try to get the birthday present back, but all the fairies are busy looking for the

decorations and trying to fix the food.
My magic has shown me that
the birthday present is hidden in Jack
Frost's Ice Castle, but I can't see exactly
where."

"We can go!" Rachel cried at once.
"We could get inside the Ice Castle and
hunt for the birthday present."

"Are you sure, girls?" asked the queen.
"It could be dangerous!"

The girls looked at each other. The Ice
Castle was a cold and scary place, but
they had been there before and knew
what to expect.

"We can't give up now," said Rachel.

"We want to do everything we can to
help," Kirsty insisted.

"Very well," said the queen with a
grateful smile.

"May I go with them, Your Majesties?" asked Belle.

"Certainly," said King Oberon. "But remember, the goblins can't be trusted. Look after each other!"

"We will!" said Belle, Rachel, and Kirsty together.

If they could find the magic birthday present, Mrs. Walker's birthday would be a happy one and Jack Frost would get his surprise party. But goblins always guarded the towers, doors, and windows of the Ice Castle. If the girls and Belle were caught, they would be in *big* trouble!

Inside the Ice Castle

Rachel, Belle, and Kirsty gazed up at Jack Frost's home. The castle was built from sheets of ice, and it gleamed menacingly. The sky was thick with dark, heavy snow clouds. Goblins marched on duty around the castle's pointed towers.

137

"How are we going to get in?" asked Rachel.

"Look!" cried Kirsty. A goblin was zooming along the road toward them on a motorcycle, pulling a large trailer. He was wearing big driving goggles and a white silk scarf.

The girls darted behind a tree.

"What's in the trailer?" Rachel wondered aloud.

"I think it's party decorations!" said Kirsty.

A gray paper streamer had come loose and was dragging on the road. Just then, the goblin looked back and noticed it. He stopped the motorcycle and jumped off to pack the streamer away.

"That's our way in!" Kirsty declared in an excited whisper.

Belle, Rachel, and Kirsty flitted over to the trailer and tucked themselves under the tarp that covered it just as the goblin started up the motorcycle again.

They couldn't see anything, but they could hear the wheels of the trailer rumbling over the icy, uneven road. Then the engine was shut off and the trailer was dragged over bumpy cobblestones.

"Where are we having the party?" asked a goblin voice.

"In the Great Hall," came the reply. "Those pesky fairies haven't showed up to help, so we have

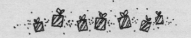

to do it all ourselves! Jack Frost's presents are already in there. We'll decorate when he isn't looking."

The girls heard the goblins walk away. When their grumbles had faded into the distance, Kirsty carefully lifted the tarp.

"All clear!" she said.

They fluttered out of the trailer and looked around. They were in the castle courtyard, which had several dark hallways leading out of it. "Let's go!" whispered Rachel. "The goblins could come back any minute!"

The three friends flew into one of
the hallways. It was narrow, cold, and
gloomy. At last, they reached a pair of tall
double doors with the words GREAT HALL
carved above them.

Suddenly, the door handles started to
turn. The girls looked around in panic.
There was nowhere to hide!

"Up!" Belle whispered urgently.

They all flew up to the ceiling and hovered there, pressing their backs against the cold roof. The doors burst open and Jack Frost stormed out. He looked up and down the hall.

"There's no one around for me to yell at!" he snarled. "Where are those goblins?"

His long, thin fingers stroked his icy chin.

"I really hate birthdays," he muttered

to himself. "So I'm going to make everyone suffer!"

He strode off, his cloak flowing behind him. As soon as he disappeared around the corner, the girls let out huge sighs of relief. They darted into the hall and closed the doors softly behind them. Jack Frost's throne stood in the center, and long tables covered with gray tablecloths lined the room. The three friends lifted the tablecloths and peered behind curtains, but all they found were cobwebs and a few bugs. No magic birthday present!

"There's one more place we haven't looked," said Rachel.

Jack Frost's throne stood on a raised platform. The girls searched along the sides of the throne and under the cushion. Then Rachel crouched down behind the throne. There was a hollow space inside the platform, and the three friends gasped when they saw what was inside.

"Presents!" said Kirsty in a breathless voice. "These must be the goblins' gifts for Jack Frost!" The girls pulled them out one by one.

"There's something else at the back,"
said Belle, peering into the darkness.

Rachel reached in, stretching her arm
as far as it would go. At last she pulled
out a little box, wrapped in shiny pink
paper and decorated with balloons.

"It's much sparklier than the others, and
it feels as light as a feather!" said Rachel,
wondering what this present could be.

Belle's eyes were bright and shining with excitement.

"That's because it's my magic birthday present!" she said. "We've found it!"

A Brave Act

Suddenly, the double doors flung open
and the girls heard a bunch of chattering
voices. Kirsty peeked around the side of
the throne.

"It's the goblins!" she exclaimed.
"They're here to decorate the hall for the
surprise party. Belle, can you use your
magic to send us back to the palace?"

Belle waved her wand . . . but nothing happened!

"Jack Frost must have put a spell on this room," she said in a worried whisper. "It means that I can't do magic until I get outside."

"We're trapped!" Rachel exclaimed.

"If we can't return the magic birthday present to the palace, the preparations for Jack Frost's party won't work," cried Belle.

"And it's only a matter of time before the goblins spot us here," added Kirsty.

She looked at her best friend in panic, but Rachel was gazing up at the tall,

pointed windows of the Great Hall.
One of them was open slightly, but
there were three goblins standing right
underneath it.

"We can't
fly out of
there,"
said Belle.
"The
goblins
would be
close
enough to
grab us."
Rachel raised
an eyebrow. "Not if they're distracted,"
she said with a little smile.

"That's it!" Kirsty exclaimed. She
turned to Belle. "Rachel and I will create

a distraction on the other side of the hall. While the goblins are looking at us, you can fly out of the window!"

Belle looked worried.

"I don't want to leave you here," she said. "It could be dangerous. What if the goblins catch you? What if Jack Frost finds you?"

"The king and queen are coming here for the surprise party," said Rachel. "We can face anything, knowing that our friends are on their way!"

Belle hugged them both.

"I think you're both really brave," she said. "Thank you! I'll be as fast as I can!"

Rachel and Kirsty each took a deep breath. Then they held hands and flew out from behind the throne, heading toward the far end of the hall.

"Hey, goblins, over here!" shouted
Kirsty.

The goblins let out howls of anger.

"It's a pair of
pesky fairies!"

"Get them!"

"Catch them!"

"Stop them!"

The goblins
all rushed to
join in the
chase, and a sea
of bony green
fingers snatched
the air near Rachel
and Kirsty. Not a single goblin noticed
Belle slip quietly out of the window. But
Rachel and Kirsty saw her go, and they
smiled at each other. Now they just had

to keep out of the goblins' way until help arrived!

The two friends flitted around the hall, dodging back and forth to keep out of the goblins' clutches. One goblin jumped onto another's shoulders and tried to grab Rachel, but she did a somersault in midair. The goblin lost his balance and crashed to the floor with a yell.

Another goblin bounced up and down on the throne cushion, and then launched himself through the air at Kirsty. She flew

to one side at
the last minute.
The goblin
hit the
dangling
chandelier
and hung there,
yelling for help. It was chaos!

"Just keep them busy!" Kirsty panted,
flying higher to escape an especially tall
goblin.

"My wings feel so tired." Rachel
gasped. "I'm not sure how much longer
I can—"

"WHAT IS GOING ON?" roared a
furious voice.

The girls screamed, and all the goblins
froze on the spot. Jack Frost was standing
in the doorway!

"Fairies!" Jack Frost hissed. "I know why you're here! You'll never find the magic birthday present."

"You're too late!" said Kirsty.

"Never!" he snarled. "I hid it far too well for you to find it!"

He lunged toward the throne.

"He'll find his presents!" squealed a goblin. "Stop him!"

Every single goblin hurled himself at

Jack Frost, who disappeared in a pile
of green arms and legs.

"Get off me!" his muffled voice yelled.
"I'll banish you all, you foolish goblins!"

"That would be a terrible mistake," said
the gentle voice of Queen Titania just
then. "They're only trying to give you a
happy birthday."

The fairies had arrived!

Parties Galore!

With a wave of the queen's wand, Jack
Frost's spell on the room was lifted.
The Great Hall was transformed into a
sparkling party scene! Fairies fluttered
in carrying frosted party food and
glittery snowflake decorations. The
gray tablecloths turned silvery blue,
and the ceiling shimmered with icicles.

The goblins scrambled to their feet and rushed to add their decorations to the room. Jack Frost stood up, scowling and smoothing out his beard.

"What do *you* want?" he snapped at the king and queen.

King Oberon stepped forward.

"Everyone deserves a very special birthday, including you," he said. "The goblins care about you, and they wanted you to have a wonderful party. We were happy to help."

Jack Frost's eyes opened very wide. His mouth fell open.

"Getting older is something to be

celebrated!" Queen Titania added.

Jack Frost looked too surprised to speak.
Then the three goblins who had
organized the party stepped proudly
forward, carrying the misshapen cake. Its
sharp, ugly spikes were frosted with blue-
silver icing, and there were candles stuck
out of it at all different angles.
Silver balls spelled out
HAPPY BIRTHDAY!
across the bottom,
and the goblins
had added a
gray ribbon at
the base as a
finishing touch.
As Jack Frost stared
at it, everyone started
to sing.

"Happy birthday to you . . ."

Once the song ended, there was a moment of silence. Then Jack Frost leaned forward, closed his eyes, and took a deep breath. After a second, he opened his eyes and blew out all the candles.

"There's something missing from this party," he said.

"Uh-oh. I hope he's not going to do anything mean," Rachel whispered.

He turned to a few of the goblins and tapped his wand on their heads. They were instantly transformed into the Gobolicious Band!

"Hooray!" shouted the goblins.

King Oberon gave a wave of his wand and a stage appeared.

"And now, a special performance from Frosty and his Gobolicious Band!" King Oberon announced with a smile.

Jack Frost pulled some sunglasses from his pocket and stepped up to the microphone.

"Maybe birthdays aren't so bad after all," he said. "Let's rock!"

It was the best party ever held in the Ice Castle. Rachel and Kirsty danced with all their fairy friends. They even tried to dance with the goblins, but the goblins kept stepping on their toes and giggling.

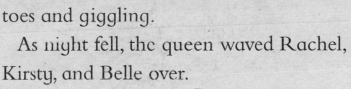

As night fell, the queen waved Rachel, Kirsty, and Belle over.

"I am so grateful to you for finding the birthday charms," she said. "Thanks to you, we were able to show Jack Frost that birthdays *can* be fun."

"We were glad to help," said Rachel, hugging Belle.

"It's time for you to be getting home," said the queen with a twinkle in her eyes. "I believe you have another party to attend!"

"My mom's birthday party!" Rachel exclaimed.

Belle hugged Rachel and Kirsty good-bye. "Thank you so much for all your help!" she said.

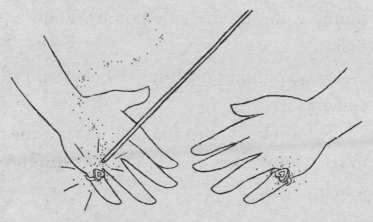

She tapped them both on the hand with her wand, and there was a sparkling flash. When the girls looked down, each of them had a heart-shaped ring on her little finger.

"Thank you!" they cried.

As they spoke, a whirl of glittering fairy dust surrounded them. They

felt themselves rising into the air and
spinning as if they were dancing.

When the sparkles faded, they were
standing outside the Tippington village
hall.

"Let's go and find Mom!" Rachel said
eagerly.

They ran back into the hall, just in time
to see Mrs. Walker opening her beautiful
jewelry box.

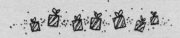

"I must have gotten the boxes mixed up!" Mr. Walker was saying. "Silly me!"

"Thank goodness," said Kirsty. "It's the perfect present!"

Rachel smiled at Kirsty and squeezed her hand.

"No gift could be better than the adventure we just had!" she said.

RAINBOW
magic
SPECIAL EDITION

Florence
the Friendship
Fairy

by Daisy Meadows

MORE
FAIRY
FUN THAN
EVER!

■SCHOLASTIC

The Fairyland Palace

Maypole

Bandstand

Stalls

Treasure Hunt

Kirsty's House

Wetherbury Village

The fairies are planning a Friendship Day
But I'll soon take their smiles away.
I'll ruin it all, I'll wreck their fun,
I'll break up the friendships one by one!

I'll steal Florence's magic things
And laugh at the misery that this act brings!
A ribbon, a book, some bracelets, too —
She really won't know what to do.

Friendship will be finished, wait and see.
Soon everyone will be friendless, just like me!

**Find the hidden letters in the stars
throughout this book. Unscramble all 10 letters
to spell two special friendship words!**

The Memory Book

Contents

Magic
Memories

Rachel Walker pulled a large scrapbook
from underneath Kirsty Tate's bed, and
the two best friends opened it between
them. It was their memory book, full of
souvenirs from all the exciting times
they'd shared together.

"That vacation on Rainspell Island
was really special," Rachel said, pointing

at the ferry tickets and map that had
been stuck into the book.

"I know," Kirsty replied, smiling. "It
was the first time we met each other —
and the first time we met the fairies,
too!" She lowered her voice. "I wonder if
we'll have a fairy adventure this week."

"I hope so," Rachel said, feeling her
heart thump excitedly at the thought.
She and her parents were spending her
school vacation with Kirsty's family, and
she had been wondering the same thing

herself. Somehow, extra-special things always seemed to happen when she and Kirsty got together!

The girls kept looking through their book. There was the museum pamphlet from the day they'd met Storm the Lightning Fairy; tickets to Strawberry Farms, where they'd helped Georgia the Guinea Pig Fairy; plus all sorts of photos, postcards, maps, petals, and leaves. . . .

Kirsty frowned when she spotted an empty space on one page. "Did a picture fall out?" she wondered.

"It must have," Rachel said. "You can see that something was stuck there before. I think it was a picture of the fairy models we painted the day we met Willow the Wednesday Fairy. I wonder where it went."

As the girls turned more pages, they realized that photo wasn't the only thing missing. A map of the constellations that Kirsty's gran had given them the night they'd helped Stephanie the Starfish Fairy had vanished, and so had the all-access pass they'd had for the Fairyland Games. Each time they turned a page, they discovered something even worse.

"Oh, no! This photo of us at Camp Stargaze is torn," Rachel said in dismay.

"This page has scribbles all over it," Kirsty cried. "How did that happen?"

"And where did *this* picture come from?" Rachel asked, pointing at a colorful image of a pretty little fairy. She had shoulder-length blond hair that was pinned back with a pink star-shaped clip. She wore a sparkly lilac top and a ruffled blue skirt with a colorful belt, and pink sparkly ankle boots. "I've never even seen her before!" She bit her lip. "Something weird is going on, Kirsty. You don't think —"

Before Rachel could finish her sentence, the picture of the fairy began to sparkle and glitter with all the colors of the rainbow. The girls watched, wide-eyed,

as the fairy fluttered her wings, stretched,
and then flew right off the page in a
whirl of twinkling dust!

"Oh!" Kirsty gasped. "Hello! What's
your name? How did you get into our
memory book?"

The fairy smiled, shook out her wings,
and flew a loop-the-loop. "I'm Florence
the Friendship Fairy," she said in a sweet

voice, her bright eyes darting around the room. "You're Kirsty and Rachel, aren't you? I've heard so much about you! I know you've been good friends to the fairies many, many times before."

"It's so nice to meet you," Rachel said. "But, Florence, do you know what happened to our memory book? Things are missing from the pages, and some things have even been ruined."

Florence fluttered over and landed on the bed. "I'm afraid that's the reason I came here," she said sadly. "Special memory books, scrapbooks, and photo albums everywhere have been ruined and stolen — so I need your help!"

Friendship and Frost!

The girls were confused, so Florence explained. "As the friendship fairy, I do my best to keep friendships strong throughout the human world and the fairy world, too," she said. "Like you, I have a memory book that I fill with my nicest friendship memories — party invitations, pressed flowers, pictures . . ."

"That sounds beautiful," Rachel said with a smile.

"It is," Florence replied. "Best of all, it's full of special friendship magic. When my book is with me, its magic protects all the special friendship mementos made and collected by friends all over the world. It also keeps the wonderful memories inside them safe! But unfortunately . . ."

"Don't tell me — Jack Frost has done something horrible again!" Kirsty said knowingly. Jack Frost was a cruel, angry creature who was always doing awful things with the help of his sneaky goblins.

"Yes," said Florence glumly. "Jack Frost doesn't believe in friendship." She frowned. "I think he's jealous of other people having best friends and doing fun things together, because he doesn't have any friends. Everyone is too scared of him."

Rachel and Kirsty nodded. They had met Jack Frost many times before, and he was scary. He was always so mean and grumpy — and he had very strong magical powers, too.

"We fairies have been planning a special Friendship Day for tomorrow,"

Florence told them. "The Party Fairies have been helping get everything ready — the music, the outfits, the party games, the food. Oh, it's going to be so much fun! But when I was in the party workshop, I put down my memory book for a minute so I could help Cherry the Cake Fairy with her icing. Before I knew what was happening, the goblins had burst in and stolen my book!"

"Oh, no!" cried Rachel. "That's awful."

"Is that why our memory book has been ruined, too?" Kirsty asked.

"Yes," Florence said. "Since my memory

book was taken, other people's books and photo albums haven't been magically protected. I'm sure the goblins have taken the chance to go around ruining as many of them as they can!"

"Well, we'll help you find your magic book," Rachel said, her eyes gleaming with excitement at the thought of another fairy adventure. "Where do you think we should start looking?"

"Oh, thank you!" Florence said. "True friends always help one another." She fluttered over to perch on Kirsty's knee. "I've been following the goblins' trail. They're definitely in the human world, and they've obviously been here in Wetherbury, since they messed up your book. So we could look around the village — do you think your parents will let you do that?"

"Yes," Kirsty replied. "Wetherbury is a small village, and I know most people here. Mom and Dad are fine with me

being out, as long as I'm with a friend
and I tell them where we're going.
Maybe if we —" She broke off as she
heard footsteps approaching. "Quick,
Florence! Hide!" she whispered urgently.

On the
Goblin Trail

With a whirl of sparkly fairy dust,
Florence fluttered her wings and flew
back into the book. She became a picture
on the page once again.

Rachel smiled. Fairy magic was so
amazing!

Kirsty's mom came into the room,
holding her purse and a shopping bag.

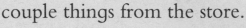

"Girls, I'm just about to do some baking for the village-hall party, but I need a couple things from the store. Would you mind —"

"We'll get them," Kirsty interrupted at once, flashing a grin at Rachel. "What do you need?"

Kirsty's mom wrote a list and opened her purse. The party she'd mentioned was being held two days later, to celebrate the reopening of the village hall. Everyone in the village had helped restore the hall to its former glory and was planning to go to the party. It sounded like it was going to be a lot of fun.

While Mrs. Tate was looking in her

purse, Florence gave Rachel a wink. She
flew out of the memory book in a flurry
of pink sparkles and fluttered to hide in
Rachel's pocket. Kirsty's mom looked up
just as the last sparkle of magic dust
disappeared — *phew!* — and gave Kirsty
some money.

The girls headed out, with Florence
peeking out of Rachel's pocket. They
hadn't gone very far when they spotted
a colorful scrap of paper blowing across
the ground. Rachel pounced on it
immediately. "Look, Kirsty, it's the ticket

to the flower show where we met Ella the Rose Fairy!" she said. "The goblins must have dropped it."

"So we know they went this way!" Kirsty said excitedly, putting the paper carefully into her bag. She looked down the street, hoping to spot a flash of goblin green. "Let's head for High Street."

The girls walked down Twisty Lane and passed the village hall. It was already decorated with strings of flags for the party, and looked brand-new with its fresh coat of paint.

As she was admiring it, Kirsty spotted something stuck in a bush near the entrance to the village hall's parking lot. "It's a candy wrapper," she said, picking it up and showing Rachel the shiny red paper. "But not an ordinary one."

"I recognize that!" Florence said eagerly. "Strawberry Sparkles — they're made by Honey the Candy Fairy!"

Rachel smiled, remembering the adventure she and Kirsty had with Honey. It had definitely been one of their

yummiest fairy missions! "That wrapper is from our memory book, too. We're still on the goblins' trail!"

The girls kept walking and were just

passing the park when they heard the
sound of grumpy voices arguing.

"Stop smiling, you look awful," one
voice complained. "And you two, stop
pushing each other."

"He keeps jabbing me," another
voice moaned. "Cut it out!"

"Ouch!"

The girls and
Florence looked
at one another.
"Sounds like
goblins!" Florence
whispered excitedly.
"Let's take a closer look."

Kirsty and Rachel slipped into the park
and hid behind a big flowering bush.
They peeked through the leaves to see

five bickering goblins. They were all
jostling one another as they posed for a
photograph.

"Ready?" called a sixth goblin.
"Say . . . UGLY!"

"UGLY!" they cried, all leering
horribly at the camera.

"Perfect," said the goblin with the
camera. "So we have a photo, some dirt,

a thistle, a few weeds . . . Our memory book is really coming along."

"Our stuff is way better than that silly fairy's," scoffed one of the other goblins. "Flowers and fairy dust and all sorts of pink stuff? Yuck!"

"Come on, let's find some more things," the tallest goblin ordered. "Put what you've collected in your pockets,

and don't forget the yucky fairy book.
Jack Frost said we weren't allowed to let
it out of our sight."

The goblins marched out of the park,
heading for High Street. One was
carrying a book with a purple and gold
cover. Florence stiffened when she saw it.

"There's my book!" she cried. "We
have to get it back. Follow those goblins!"

Boo!

Kirsty and Rachel hung back until the goblins were a safe distance away, then followed them along Twisty Lane. The goblins all seemed like they were in very good moods. They kept stopping to take photographs of one another! But these photos weren't like ones in ordinary memory books or albums — instead, the goblins took pictures of the strangest things.

"Take one of me with this great big snail!" one goblin cried eagerly, picking up a large snail and  balancing it on his head. "It's so nice and slimy!"

"Take one of us having a fight," another goblin suggested, as he elbowed a skinny goblin with knobby knees.

"Hey, cut it out!" yelled the skinny goblin.

Click! Click! went the camera at the snail, the fight, and then a pile of garbage that another goblin found.

"Ahh, this is what good memories are all about," said the smallest goblin, who had mean, squinty eyes. "Hey, what about a photo of me ripping up this silly fairy book? That would be great!"

Florence gasped as he grabbed the memory book. It looked like he was going to tear it with his warty green fingers! "No!" she cried, zooming through the air before Kirsty or Rachel could stop her. "Don't do that!"

The goblins spun around at the sound
of her little voice. "Oh, great," the tallest
one moaned. "Just what we *didn't* want.
A silly fairy, here to ruin everything.
Quick, run!"

The goblins sprinted away. The small
goblin was still holding Florence's
precious memory book!
As he ran, pretty
flowers and
sparkly
treasures
dropped
from its
pages.
Florence
looked like she
wanted to cry!

"They're ruining it!" she wailed,
swooping down and waving her magic
wand to make
all the items
fairy-size.
She collected
everything
that had fallen
out of her
memory book.

Meanwhile,
the goblins were getting
away. The girls didn't want to lose sight
of them! "Florence, could you use your
magic to turn us into fairies?" Kirsty
asked, thinking fast. "That way we can
fly after the goblins."

"Good idea," Florence said, pointing

her wand at the girls and whispering
some magic words.

Instantly, a stream of bright sparkles
flew out from her wand and swirled all
around Kirsty and Rachel. Then they
were shrinking smaller and smaller — and
they had their own shining fairy wings
on their backs. Even Kirsty's shopping
bag had shrunk down to fairy-size!

Luckily, nobody was around to see them as the three fairies flew up into the air and began zooming after the goblins.

"We need a plan," Rachel said thoughtfully. In the distance, the goblins had reached a row of stores and had slowed down. They obviously thought they'd gotten away from the fairies.

"If we could somehow get that small goblin to drop the book . . ." Kirsty said, thinking aloud. "Maybe we can make him jump, and he might let go of it?"

"And then I could use my magic to shrink it back to fairy-size, and fly in to grab it!" Florence finished.

The three friends smiled at one another. "We could fly up behind the goblins so that we're really close to them," Rachel suggested. "Then Florence could turn us

back into girls, and we could shout really loudly. That should make them jump!"

Kirsty giggled. "It would make *me* jump," she said. "Come on, let's try it."

Silently, the fairies flew as close to the goblins as they dared. Luckily, the goblins had their backs turned. They were busy peering into the candy shop, moaning that there weren't any bogmallows inside. When Kirsty and Rachel were hovering just behind the

goblin holding Florence's memory book, Florence waved her wand and turned them back into girls.

"BOO!" Rachel and Kirsty shouted at the top of their lungs.

"Aarrrgh!" screamed the goblins, turning around in fear. But unfortunately, the smallest goblin didn't drop the book as they'd hoped. In fact, he only clutched it tighter — and all the goblins ran off down the street!

A Tempting Offer

"After them!" cried Florence, flying through the air like a streak of light. Kirsty and Rachel followed on foot, running as fast as they could.

The goblins ducked down an alley, with Florence and the girls right behind them. Kirsty grinned as she realized that the alley was a dead end. Soon, the goblins would be trapped!

Sure enough, the goblins realized there was nowhere else to run. They stopped and turned, their backs against the wall.

The smallest goblin hid the memory book behind him, a determined gleam in his eye. "You're not getting this back," he said rudely.

"I don't know why you want *my* memory book, anyway," Florence said. "You goblins hate pink sparkly things. Wouldn't you rather have a nice green memory book of your own?"

"Well, yes," the tallest goblin said, shrugging. "But we don't have one. So we're taking yours instead."

This gave Rachel an idea. "But if we could find you the perfect goblin memory book with a gorgeous green cover, would you . . . trade?" she asked, crossing her fingers behind her back.

The goblins looked at one another, but none of them said anything.

Kirsty tried to hide her smile. It was obvious — they *did* want their own book!

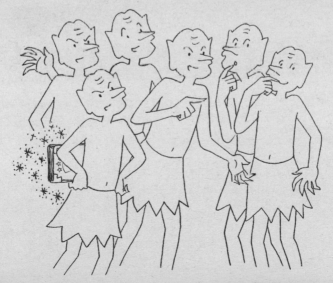

"Florence, would you be able to use your
magic to make a new memory book for
the goblins?" she asked.

"Of course!" Florence said. She smiled
at the goblins. "I could make one that
would be exactly what you wanted.
Maybe the cover could have thorns on it,
or slimy patches . . ."

"Oooh!" the goblins cried, their eyes
lighting up.

"I'd make the pages green, too,"
Florence went on. "And I'd even add
some special magic so that you can
add your favorite smells to the book —
IF you give me my book back."

"Favorite *smells*," the knobby-kneed
goblin said longingly. "We could put in
the smell of moldy toadstools."

"And stinky feet!" another suggested.
All of the goblins looked at one
another. "It's a deal!" they chorused.

"Hooray!" cheered Kirsty, Rachel, and
Florence. The little fairy got to work
right away. She waved her wand and
muttered some magic words. Seconds
later, a big green book appeared in the
tallest goblin's hands. It was oozing with
some yucky-smelling slime, and had a
sticky, prickly cover.

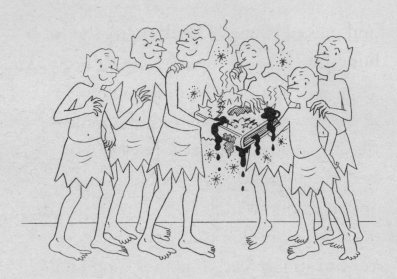

"Oh," said the tallest goblin, stroking the book. "It's so ugly. It's perfect!" He turned to the smallest goblin. "Go ahead, hand over her book," he ordered. "This is worth *fifty* silly fairy memory books!"

The smallest goblin thrust Florence's memory book toward the little fairy. With a smile of delight, she waved her wand, and it shrank to fairy-size in the goblin's hand. Then she fluttered down and picked it up. "Thank you," she said happily.

The goblins wandered off, excitedly discussing what smells they'd add to their new book and how Jack Frost would love their horrid handiwork.

"Take your time," Florence called after them. "Memory books, like true friendships, can't be rushed!" Then she smiled at Kirsty and Rachel. "And now it's time to repair my memory book — and all the others that have been ruined!"

She touched her wand to her memory book. Bright, shimmering waves of magic began to pulse from it, spreading through the air in sparkling ripples of light.

"There," she said happily, as the last light flickered and disappeared. "Everything should be fixed, and your memory book will be full again." She smiled. "Thanks, both of you," she said, fluttering over to give the girls tiny fairy kisses. "I'd better go back to Fairyland now, to finish getting everything ready for tomorrow's Friendship Day. See you soon, I hope! Oh, and maybe you should take a look in that shopping bag?"

"In the shopping bag?" Kirsty asked, glancing down at the empty canvas bag that still hung from her arm.

"Bye!" Florence called mischievously, vanishing.

Kirsty opened the bag and peeked inside. Then she smiled.

"What is it?" Rachel asked, trying to see.

Kirsty pulled out two pink invitations with their names written in silver ink. *"You are invited to the fairies' Friendship Day at the Fairyland Palace,"* she read, beaming. "Oh, Rachel! How exciting!"

"Hooray!" Rachel cheered, hugging Kirsty happily. She grinned as they began walking toward the stores. "I knew this was going to be another good vacation together, Kirsty. I just knew it!"

The Friendship
Ribbon

Contents

Party Preparations

"Good morning, everyone!" Mrs. Tate said to the gathered crowd. "And thank you so much for offering to help out. There's a lot to do!"

It was the next day, and Kirsty and Rachel had come to the village hall with Kirsty's mom and a group of villagers. They were all there to help with preparations for the grand reopening party.

The hall had recently been redecorated, with the whole community's help. It was being renamed the Wetherbury Friendship Hall.

"We have balloons, streamers, and ribbons to sort through and hang up," Mrs. Tate said, "music to organize, lights to arrange . . . Oh, and the banner! Kirsty and Rachel, would you help me unroll it, please?"

Rachel, Kirsty, and her mom carefully unrolled the large white banner, until everyone could see what was written on

it: WELCOME TO THE WETHERBURY
FRIENDSHIP HALL!

"It doesn't look very exciting at the
moment, but I brought some colorful
paints," Mrs. Tate went on. "And since this
party is all about friendship and working
together, I thought it would be nice if lots
of different people could each paint in a
letter of the banner," she explained.
"That way, it'll look really bright and
eye-catching. OK? Let's get started!"

The team of helpers immediately got to
work — some blowing up balloons,

others untangling the long strings of ribbon and sparkly strands of lights.

"Should we paint our letters on the banner first?" Kirsty asked Rachel.

"Good idea," Rachel said. "Let's take it into one of the side rooms, so it won't get in anyone's way."

The girls carried the banner and paint into a smaller room off the main hall. The room had a piano at one end, and lots of chairs stacked up along the walls. They spread the banner out on the floor, then chose their colors and brushes. Kirsty took the pink paint, while Rachel

decided on purple. Then both girls carefully filled in one letter each.

"This is going to look great when everyone's painted their letters," Rachel said, admiring their work.

"Definitely," said Kirsty with a smile. She was just about to go and wash out her paintbrush when she heard a tiny sigh of relief from behind her.

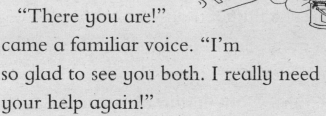

"There you are!" came a familiar voice. "I'm so glad to see you both. I really need your help again!"

Both girls turned to see Florence the Friendship Fairy flying through an open window, her pretty face looking pale and anxious.

"What happened?" Rachel asked. "Are you OK?"

Florence fluttered down to land on the jar of green paint, her wings drooping. "No, not really," she said sadly. "Today is the fairies' Friendship Day, but everything is going wrong . . . and it's the goblins' fault again! They ran off with my friendship ribbon. If I don't get it back, the party will be a disaster!" She sighed. "Can you come to Fairyland with me and help look for it?"

"Of course!" Kirsty said at once. Then she paused and bit her lip. "The only thing is, we're supposed to be helping my mom here."

"Don't worry," Florence said. "Time will stand still in the human world while you're with me in Fairyland. Is that all right?"

Rachel nodded, her eyes lighting up at the thought of another fairy adventure. "Perfect," she replied.

Florence smiled. "Then let's go — there's no time to lose!"

Off to Fairyland!

Florence waved her wand and a stream
of pink sparkles swirled all around Rachel
and Kirsty, lifting them off the ground
in a glittering whirlwind. The room
became a blur of colors before their eyes!
They felt themselves spinning through the
air, growing smaller and smaller
and smaller. . . .

A few minutes later, their feet touched the ground, and the sparkly whirlwind slowly vanished. Kirsty realized that they were on the grounds of the Fairyland Palace. Lots of fairies she recognized were busily working away. The girls were back in Fairyland — and they were fairies now, too, with their own shimmering wings!

Rachel beamed at Kirsty. Fairyland was the most exciting place ever!

"Look, there's Polly the Party Fun Fairy," she said, pointing as she spotted the little blond fairy across the courtyard. "Oh, and Melodie the Music Fairy, too."

Polly appeared to be working on a new party game that involved teams of fairies competing to fly up and collect glittering gold stars from a nearby tree. Melodie was busy listening to the Music Fairies

rehearse. But both fairies seemed to be having problems!

Florence bit her lip anxiously as Polly's fairies bumped into one another in mid-air and crashed to the ground with surprised shouts. Melodie put her head in her hands at the squeaks and squawks the musicians were making.

"Oh, no." Florence sighed. "Things are still no better here. We have to find my friendship ribbon! Without it, the party is going to be awful."

"What *is* the friendship ribbon?" Kirsty asked, confused.

Florence opened her mouth to reply, but then gave a shout of warning instead. "Phoebe! Watch out!"

Rachel and Kirsty turned to see Phoebe the Fashion Fairy pushing a rack of gorgeous party dresses along a cobbled path nearby. The clothing rack was bouncing on the cobblestones, and some of the dresses and accessories had slipped off their hangers onto the ground without

Phoebe realizing. Phoebe heard Florence's shout and spotted the fallen items. Before she could pick them up, Zoe the Skating Fairy zoomed up behind her carrying a huge box . . . and roller-skated right over the dresses, completely ruining them!

"Oh, no!" Phoebe wailed in dismay. "My dresses!"

Zoe skidded around to see what had happened, and threw up her hands in

horror — dropping the box she'd been carrying. It landed with a crash. "Oh, no!" she echoed. "Your dresses — and the best royal china plates — are ruined!"

Florence looked like she wanted to cry. "This is getting worse and worse!" she said. She turned back to Kirsty and Rachel. "The friendship ribbon is always tied to the maypole," she explained, pointing to where a tall golden pole

stood in the center of the lawn. The three
fairies fluttered over to it. "While it's
there, it means that friends can work
together well, and have fun. It was going
to be used in a special friendship dance
around the maypole tonight — but the
goblins saw the ribbon and decided *they*
wanted to play with it. And ever since

they took it down, things have been
going all wrong."

"We'll help you find the ribbon,"
Rachel promised her. "Come on, let's
start looking for it — and those sneaky
goblins, too!"

Goblin Games

Florence, Kirsty, and Rachel fluttered up into the air and flew above the palace grounds, keeping a lookout for any signs of goblins below. They passed the bakery, where it smelled as if something was burning. Then they flew over the party-decoration workshop.

Grace the Glitter Fairy had just accidentally knocked over a huge barrel

of sequins, which poured out in a sparkling flood all over the floor. "Oh, *no*!" they heard her cry in exasperation. Florence had told them that the friendship ribbon was long, bright blue, and covered in stars. As the three friends flew past the palace stables and across the lake, there was no sign of it — or the goblins — anywhere.

"Let's try looking in here," Florence suggested, pointing to a small wooded area up ahead. Kirsty and Rachel followed their fairy friend as she swooped between the shady trees.

Birds sang sweetly and a light breeze rustled the leaves as the three fairies flew through the woods. Then Florence landed abruptly and turned, putting a finger to her lips before ducking behind a large tree trunk. Rachel and Kirsty could hear muffled shouts and cheers. They

hurried to hide behind trees of their own as they realized that there was a group of goblins gathered in a clearing up ahead. Peering around their trees, they could see that six goblins were playing with the magic ribbon — using it as a sparkly jump rope at first, and then as a rope for tug-of-war.

Florence's eyes were wide with alarm.

"They better not rip my ribbon!" she
murmured. "I can't bear to watch!"

The goblins were split into two teams
of three for the game. Eventually, one
team pulled the others over a branch on
the ground that they were using as a
marker.

"We win!" cried the tallest goblin on
the winning team. He let go of the
ribbon to celebrate with his teammates.

Then he taunted the other team. "Losers! Losers!"

"Your team *cheated*!" argued a frowning goblin on the other team, putting his hands on his hips. "That's not fair. I don't want to be friends with you anymore."

The two goblins started fighting, and another goblin had to break them up. "Hey, stop it! This is supposed to be our Friendship Party," he reminded them. "Anything the fairies can do, we can do better — right?"

"Right," muttered the tall goblin.

"How about a game of blind goblin's buff?" the smallest goblin suggested. "We can use the ribbon as a blindfold."

Florence beckoned Kirsty and Rachel behind a shrub while the goblins began arguing over who was going to be the blind goblin first. "I really need to get that ribbon from them," she whispered, "but I don't know how we can. They keep using it in all their games!"

Kirsty nodded. "They're really enjoying playing with it, aren't they?" she murmured.

The girls watched as the smallest goblin

ended the argument about who would be
blindfolded first by tying the ribbon
quickly around his own head. The other
goblins dodged him, giggling as he
blundered around, arms outstretched,
trying to catch one of them.

But the goblins didn't play nicely for
very long. One of them picked up a stick
and used it to jab the blindfolded goblin
in the ribs.

"Ow!" he yelped, flailing around. The others cracked up laughing.

Then another one of the goblins threw a handful of acorns at the blindfolded one. He cried out in surprise as they *ping*ed off his pointy nose. "Stop it!" he yelled, running toward the noise of the other goblins' cackles. "Stop!"

Rachel, Kirsty, and Florence, meanwhile, were still trying to come up with a plan to get the ribbon. It was hard to think straight, with the noise of the squabbling goblins in the background. Then Kirsty smiled. "I have an idea!" she whispered.

Ribbons for Racing

"Florence, could you use your magic to make some other ribbons that look the same as the friendship ribbon?" Kirsty asked.

Florence nodded. "Of course," she said. "They won't be quite as sparkly as the friendship ribbon, but —"

"That's fine," Kirsty said, interrupting. "In fact, that's perfect! Let's tell the goblins that a three-legged race is the only way to tell who are the best friends. We can use the ribbons to tie up their legs. Hopefully they'll be so distracted by the race that we'll be able to sneak up, take the friendship ribbon, and fly off!"

Florence grinned. "I love it!" she said.

She waved her wand and spoke some magic words under her breath. Then, in a swirl of pink sparkles, two matching ribbons appeared in her hand.

"There!" She smiled. "Now let's put our plan into action."

Rachel, Kirsty, and Florence all fluttered into the clearing, just as the smallest goblin ripped off his blindfold. "I'm not playing this game anymore," he grumbled. "You guys are so mean! You're the worst friends ever!"

"Uh-oh," Rachel said loudly. "Worst friends ever? That's not good. We were just wondering which of you are *best* friends."

The goblins all replied at once, pointing as they talked. "I'm best friends with him, but he likes *him* better than me."

"I don't like him or him or him, but *he's* OK, I guess."

"I'm the best at everything, so I must be the best friend," another boasted.

"Well," Kirsty said over their chatter, "what about having a competition to decide who are the best friends of all? We have some extra ribbons here, so you can have a three-legged race. Get into pairs as quickly as you can!"

Kirsty spoke so firmly that the goblins all scurried to find a partner and tie their legs together.

"The first pair to reach the weeping willow tree wins!" Rachel said. "Ready, set, GO!"

The goblins began hobbling off in pairs, all looking very determined. But as they ran, Kirsty began to doubt that her plan would work. The goblins were

actually all really good at running three-legged! Would *any* of them fall over?

"Hmmm," said Florence, as if reading Kirsty's mind. "Maybe I should make things a little trickier for them. . . ." She waved her wand and whispered some more magic words. A stream of sparkles swirled out of her wand tip. Suddenly, lots of stones and acorns rolled in front of the goblins' feet!

"Ooh! Ahh!" wailed the goblins. One by one, they stumbled and fell on top of one another!

They weren't hurt, but the goblins were soon a big tangle of arms and legs, all shouting and arguing.

"Quick!" Rachel urged. "Now's our chance to get the ribbon!"

Party Time!

Florence didn't need to be told twice! She zoomed through the air and untied the sparkliest ribbon from the tangle of goblin legs, then fluttered up high. "Got it!" she cheered. "Come on, let's fly back and tie it to the maypole!"

Rachel and Kirsty soared into the air after Florence, and the three of them flew

all the way back to the palace grounds.
There, Florence tied the magic ribbon
back on the maypole. "Hooray!" they
cheered, hugging one another in
triumph.

"Is that Kirsty and Rachel I see?"
came a booming voice. The girls turned
to see the fairy king and queen walking
into the courtyard with big smiles on
their faces.

Rachel and Kirsty smiled back politely
and dipped into curtsies.

King Oberon and Queen Titania were always really nice, but the girls still felt shy in front of them. "Hello," they said together.

Florence flew down from the maypole. "Kirsty and Rachel have helped me twice in the last two days, Your Majesties," she said. "Yesterday they helped me get my magic memory book from the goblins, and today they helped rescue the friendship ribbon. They are true friends to the fairies!"

Queen Titania smiled and nodded.

"Girls, we would be honored if you two could declare our Friendship Party officially open," she said. She waved her wand, and the sound of a bell ringing majestically echoed through the air. All the fairies fell silent and turned to see what was happening.

Holding hands, Rachel and Kirsty looked at each other and then said, "We declare the fairy Friendship Party officially . . . OPEN!"

A great cheer rose as the celebrations began. Melodie and her orchestra played some beautiful music, while another group of fairies performed a special friendship dance around the maypole. Then everyone went into the Great Hall of the palace for some party games with Polly. Grace the Glitter Fairy had decorated the hall with the most wonderful pink and silver streamers!

Rachel and Kirsty had a fantastic time! Polly's new party games were a lot of fun. They played Best Friend Hide-and-Seek, joined in some obstacle-course races and a treasure hunt, and then took a Best Friend Fun Quiz. It was wonderful to see so many of their fairy friends again, especially since everyone was enjoying themselves so much!

A little later, Cherry the Cake Fairy and Honey the Candy Fairy made all sorts of delicious food appear. Kirsty and Rachel couldn't wait to try Cherry's delicious rose-and-lavender cupcakes, and Honey's Fairy Fizz Drops and

Magic Marshmallow Melts. "Delicious,"
Kirsty said, licking her lips. "Thank you,
Honey. Those are the yummiest candies
I've ever tasted!"

"And the fluffiest cupcakes, too,"
Rachel said, smiling at Cherry. "What
a great Friendship Party this is!"

Just then, King Oberon and Queen
Titania appeared beside the girls. "Thanks
again for everything you've done for the
fairies," the king said. "I'm afraid we need
to send you back to your world now, but
I hope you'll be back before too long."

Florence flew over to say good-bye.

"Thanks from me, too," she said. "It's wonderful to be friends with you!"

"It's wonderful to be friends with *all* of you," Kirsty replied, her eyes shining.

"See you soon, I hope," Rachel said. The queen pointed her wand at them and spoke a magic command. Golden fairy dust billowed from her wand, spinning around the girls and whisking them away in a glittering whirlwind. Seconds later, they were back in the village hall, next to the banner and paints. But something was different.

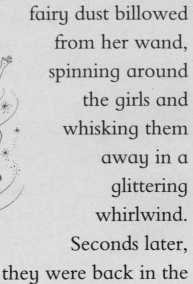

"Look, Kirsty!" Rachel whispered in delight. She pointed to the letters they'd painted on the banner, and Kirsty's eyes widened. The pink letter she'd painted was now edged with shiny gold paint, and Rachel's purple letter had been patterned with tiny silver hearts.

"Fairy magic," Kirsty said with a smile. "Don't they look pretty?"

At that moment, Mrs. Tate came into the room. "Nice work, girls," she said, when she saw they'd been painting. Then she took a closer look. "Wow!" she exclaimed. "Those letters are beautiful. You did such a great job!"

Rachel and Kirsty exchanged a secret

smile. They knew they couldn't take all the credit for the painting. Fairy magic had made their letters look extra-special — but the two friends weren't about to tell Mrs. Tate that!

The Friendship Bracelets

Contents

Village Celebrations

"Hold still! There," said Kirsty Tate, zipping up the dress her best friend, Rachel Walker, was wearing.

"Thanks." Rachel smiled. "I'm really looking forward to this party, Kirsty!"

The two girls were in Kirsty's bedroom, getting ready for a special celebration in Wetherbury, where Kirsty lived.

A year earlier, the Wetherbury Village Hall had closed because it needed a lot of repairs. Since then, a team of volunteers had worked hard to rebuild parts of the hall. They had put on a new roof and redecorated the building from top to bottom. Now, at last, it was finished! It had been renamed the Wetherbury

Friendship Hall in honor of the great teamwork that had gone into it. Kirsty's mom had helped organize a big party for the villagers and all their friends that night, to mark the hall's reopening.

Rachel and her family had come to

stay with the Tates for school break, so they were going to the party, too. And, best of all, Rachel and Kirsty were in the middle of another fairy adventure! Florence the Friendship Fairy looked after special friendships in both Fairyland and the human world. But, as usual, mean Jack Frost and his goblins were determined to ruin things!

So far, the girls had helped Florence get her magical memory book and her special friendship ribbon back, after they had been stolen by the goblins. They hoped that all of Florence's magic was safe and sound now.

The party was in full swing when Kirsty, Rachel, and their families arrived at the hall. The girls had helped decorate the main room earlier. It looked wonderful, with pink and red streamers and matching balloons. Rachel and Kirsty knew there

would be lots of games later — a treasure
hunt, a cookout, and even a magician!

"Wow, this is great," Rachel said.

"It is," Kirsty agreed. "But nobody
really seems to be enjoying themselves. I
wonder why?"

Rachel looked closer. To her surprise, she could see angry expressions on some kids' faces! Nearby, two boys glared at each other. "There's no way football is better than baseball," one snarled.

"You don't know what you're talking about!"

Other kids with grumpy faces sat on the chairs lining the room, not speaking to anyone.

Mr. and Mrs. Tate didn't seem to notice, so they took Rachel's parents off to introduce them to some other friends. Kirsty and Rachel hovered at the edge of the party, wondering what was going on. "I have a feeling that something is wrong," Kirsty said.

"It's awful, isn't it?" came a little voice from behind them. "I'm so glad you're here!"

Florence Flies In!

Kirsty and Rachel turned to see a tiny fairy peeking out from behind one of the nearby balloons. It was Florence the Friendship Fairy!

"Hello again, girls," she said. "I'm afraid I need your help one more time." Her shoulders drooped, and she suddenly looked upset. "I think it's all my fault that friends aren't getting along at this party!"

"I'm sure it's not," Kirsty said, feeling sorry for poor Florence. "Why don't we go somewhere quieter, and you can tell us what happened?"

Florence agreed and fluttered under Kirsty's hair so that she would stay hidden. The girls went outside and around to the back of the hall, where nobody could see them.

Florence flitted out from her hiding place and perched on some ivy growing up the wall. "You've helped me so much over the last couple days," she began, "and I know how many times you've helped the other fairies, too. We all really value your friendship."

Rachel felt a happy glow. "We love being friends with you all, too," she said.

Florence smiled. "I'm glad to hear it," she said. "I wanted to give you each a special friendship bracelet as a gift, to say thank you. So after our Friendship Party last night, I asked the Rainbow Fairies to contribute strands of colored thread to the bracelets. When I had the seven colors of the rainbow, I added an extra gold thread that was full of my special friendship magic. Then I wove them all together into two bracelets."

"Ooh, how pretty!" Kirsty exclaimed.

Florence's face fell. "They were pretty," she replied. "I even worked in some extra-special wishing magic that would grant you both a wish when you were wearing the bracelets. But unfortunately, Jack Frost overheard me telling the Rainbow Fairies about my plans. He didn't want you to have the bracelets, so he ordered his goblins to steal them from my workshop."

"How mean!" Rachel said. "Why doesn't he want us to have them?"

"Maybe he wanted to punish you, because you helped me get the memory book and the friendship ribbon back from his goblins," Florence said sadly. "And you know how cold and cruel he is. He doesn't understand friendship, or wanting to do nice things for  other people. He doesn't have many friends himself."

"That's true," Kirsty said thoughtfully. Jack Frost had lots of goblins under his command, but you couldn't really call them friends. "So, does Jack Frost have the bracelets now?"

"No," Florence said. "Those goblins are so sneaky, they decided to have some fun before they took the bracelets to Jack Frost. They heard about this party in Wetherbury and didn't want to miss out, so they came along. And that's the problem."

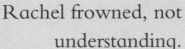

Rachel frowned, not understanding. "What do you mean?"

"Well, the goblins have the friendship bracelets," Florence went on. "But they don't realize that a friendship bracelet should only be worn by the person it was made for. If someone else wears it, my friendship magic works in reverse! Then the wearer, and anyone near the wearer, starts arguing and breaking up their friendships."

"So that's why we saw people arguing earlier," Kirsty said. "By stealing our bracelets and wearing them here, the goblins are causing everyone to fight with their friends!"

"Exactly," Florence replied sadly. "And I have to stop them before they ruin the whole party. Will you help me find the goblins, and get your bracelets back?"

"Of course," Rachel said right away. "Let's start looking!"

The three friends went back into the village hall. People were dancing, and Kirsty and Rachel peered closely at them. Some kids had put on costumes for the occasion. The dance floor was so crowded that it was hard to make out everybody's faces.

Just then, Rachel noticed two boys heading out onto the dance floor, bickering loudly.

They were both in costumes — one was dressed as a pirate, the other as a knight — but there was no mistaking their long noses and pointy ears. They were goblins!

That's
Magic!

"There they are!" Rachel whispered, pointing at the goblins as they stomped across the room. They were arguing about who was the best dancer. Both goblins started dancing to prove that they were better, though they still looked very grouchy.

All around the goblins, new arguments began springing up — silly arguments, at that! "Short hair is better than long hair," one girl snapped at another, who had a long braid. "I don't want to be friends with anyone with long hair."

"I don't like your T-shirt — so I don't like you!" one boy muttered to another.

"This is getting worse by the minute!" Florence groaned. "I'm going to try sprinkling some friendship magic around. Hopefully it will help patch up these arguments."

Kirsty and Rachel watched as Florence flew high up in the air. They saw her wave her wand, and then streams of pink stars swirled across the room.

"Sorry," the girl with short hair said to the girl with the braid. "I don't know what I was talking about. Your hair is really pretty."

"I didn't mean to be rude about your

T-shirt," the boy said to his friend. "Let's go outside and play, OK?"

"Florence's magic is working!" Kirsty said happily.

"But so is the magic from the bracelets," Rachel said. "Look!"

It was true. As fast as Florence helped friends make up, new arguments started. The two goblins were still bickering, too. As the pirate goblin shoved the knight, the sleeve of his pirate shirt rode up —

 and Kirsty noticed a rainbow-colored bracelet on his wrist. A-ha! "There's one of the bracelets," she

whispered to Rachel. "But how can we get it back?"

Before Rachel could reply, the band finished their song. The singer made an announcement. "We're going to take a break now, but a very special guest will be entertaining you while we're away. Here's . . . Milo the Magician!"

A big "Ooooh!" of excitement went up as a man in a cape and top hat walked onstage.

Everyone hurried to grab a chair, including the goblins, and sat down to watch the show. Rachel and Kirsty sat near the back of the hall, with Florence hidden under Kirsty's hair.

"There!" Florence said suddenly, pointing. Kirsty and Rachel leaned forward and counted one, two, THREE goblins sitting in the front row. One wore the pirate costume, one the knight outfit, and the third wore a tall wizard's hat and cloak.

"Oh, no," Rachel said. "Three goblins and two bracelets — this could get tricky."

The magician's show began, and the girls watched curiously. He plucked oranges from behind people's ears and pulled a rabbit from his hat. Kirsty and Rachel thought he was great! Unfortunately, the other kids in the audience were grumpy and restless, glaring at one another. The goblins all seemed to enjoy the tricks, though. They clapped enthusiastically throughout the performance.

When Milo's show ended, Mrs. Tate stepped onto the stage. "We're going to start a game of hide-and-seek now, out in the yard," she said. "Follow me, everyone!"

Most people — including the pirate and the knight goblins — hurried after Kirsty's mom. But the goblin with the wizard's hat stayed where he was. "I want more magic!" he said to Milo, who was packing up his equipment.

"Sorry," Milo said. "Show's over —

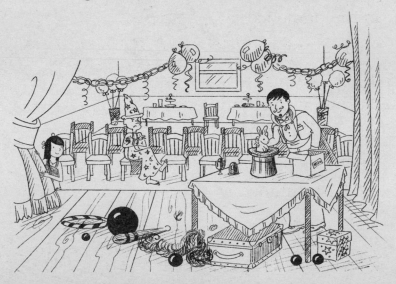

even for wizards. Why don't you go outside with the others?"

The goblin didn't budge. "I want more magic," he repeated. As he did, the girls spotted a brightly colored stripe on one of his wrists — the second friendship bracelet!

"I have an idea," Kirsty said excitedly. "If the goblin wants a magic show, maybe *we* could give him one. Then we could use some real magic to get the bracelet away from him!"

Florence grinned. "Let's give it a try!" she said.

Tricks . . . and Treasure!

Milo left the hall, but the goblin stayed right where he was, glaring into space. "Perfect," Florence said. "It's time for us to put on our very own show."

Florence waved her wand, and the girls were suddenly wearing magician costumes — capes, hats, and wands!

"Hi," Rachel said, strolling up in front of the goblin. "You like magic, huh? Want to see another show?"

The goblin blinked in surprise. "Where did you come from?" he asked.

Kirsty tapped her nose mysteriously as she walked up to join Rachel. "Magic," she said. "Now let's see . . . what's this egg doing here?"

She reached behind the goblin's pointy right ear and hoped with all her heart that Florence would be able to help her with the trick! Yes — a smooth egg appeared in her palm at just the right

moment. She drew her hand back to show the goblin what was in it.

"Wow!" Rachel said, trying not to laugh at the goblin's startled expression. "Didn't your parents ever teach you to wash behind your ears?"

"Do some more!" the goblin urged. "More magic!"

Kirsty pulled off her top hat, and showed the goblin that it was empty. "Nothing in there, right?" she said. "But

let's see what happens when I say the
magic words . . . *bibble bobble, bibble bobble!*"

The goblin gasped — and so did Kirsty.
As she finished the magic words, a
beautiful white dove flew straight out
of her hat and through
the open window.
"Whoa!"
the goblin
cried.
"You're
even better
than Milo!"
"And now
for another trick," Rachel announced.
"This may look like an ordinary wand,"
she said, tapping it against the goblin's
wizard hat. "But if I throw it up in the
air and catch it, it turns into . . ." She

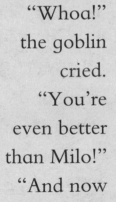

held her breath and threw the wand up high. There was a sparkle of pink magic dust. Then a string of colorful silk handkerchiefs shot out of the end of the wand — and started to wrap themselves tightly around the goblin!

"Oooh!" the goblin cried. "That was a good one!"

Kirsty and Rachel watched as the handkerchiefs wound around and around the goblin. Soon he couldn't clap anymore, since his arms were bound tight against his body. The excited light vanished from his eyes. "Hey!" he said. "What's happening?"

"This!" replied Kirsty, as she quickly untied the friendship bracelet from his wrist. "Thank you very much!"

The goblin's mouth fell open as he realized that he'd been tricked. "You — you —" he stuttered. "You horrible magicians! That's not fair!"

"I didn't think it was very fair when you and your friends stole my bracelets, either," Florence said, flying down and landing on Rachel's shoulder.

The goblin made a furious growling noise and stumbled away. "I'll make sure you don't get the other bracelet," he called. "So there!"

Kirsty and Rachel admired the friendship bracelet in Kirsty's hand. It had KIRSTY stitched across it in tiny gold letters. "Here, let me put it on for you," Florence said with a smile. She waved her wand, so that both magician costumes vanished — and the bracelet tied itself neatly around Kirsty's wrist. "Ta-da!"

"It's beautiful," Kirsty said happily. "Thank you so much, Florence. Now

we just need to get Rachel's bracelet back."

"Let's go see what those other goblins are up to," Florence said. She hid in the front pocket of Rachel's bag, and the girls headed outside.

As they walked out the front doors, they almost ran right into the goblins! The wizard goblin had been untied, and they all looked very smug. "Looking for the bracelet, are you?" the knight goblin said. "Ha! You'll never find it now."

"Yeah," the pirate goblin gloated, showing them his bare wrists. "We've hidden it somewhere really good."

"Listen up, everyone!" Kirsty's mom called just then. "While the grown-ups get the grill started, there's going to be a treasure hunt. There's real treasure at the end, in an actual treasure chest!"

The goblins looked at one another in horror. "What . . . what does the treasure chest look like?" the pirate goblin croaked after a moment.

"It's a small gold box," Mrs. Tate
replied.

The goblins all looked completely
dismayed about something. Rachel
elbowed Kirsty. "I bet they hid the
bracelet in the treasure chest!" she

guessed. "That's why they look so worried!"

"I think you're right," Kirsty said excitedly. "So we have to find the treasure chest before they do!"

The Hunt Is On!

"Here's the first clue," Mrs. Tate told the group. *"Use two sticks to tap on my top, I make a* bang — *but I'm quiet if you stop!"*

Kirsty solved the clue very quickly. "Two sticks to tap on my top . . . It's a drum," she whispered to Rachel. "It must be the drum that the band used. Come on!"

Kirsty and Rachel began running toward the hall.

"We have to get to the treasure chest first, so we can take the bracelet out before anyone else sees it," Rachel said, panting as they ran. "But how are we going to do that?"

"By flying, of course," Florence said, popping her head out of Rachel's bag. "Find somewhere quiet, and I'll turn you both into fairies!"

Kirsty veered away from the stage and ducked into the bathroom, with Rachel close behind. Florence waved her wand, sending more of her glittering fairy dust spinning all around them. Seconds later, they were fairies! The girls fluttered their wings and flew back into the hall just in time to hear a boy reading the second clue aloud.

"*We're bright and colorful, and filled with air. Tied to a string, the next clue is there. . . .*" he said, frowning.

"Bright and colorful? Sounds like flowers," one girl said eagerly.

Kirsty, Rachel, and Florence, who were perched on one of the ceiling beams, exchanged smiles. "Balloons!" they all said together. "Quick, let's go!"

They soared out into the yard. There was a big bunch of balloons tied to a tree, and they swooped down to land in the middle of them. The third clue was

attached to the string of one of the balloons! This clue led them to the front door of the hall. There, they spotted a large metal mailbox attached to the inside of the door — and what was that, poking out of it?

"It's the treasure chest!" Rachel cheered in excitement.

Kirsty opened the mailbox flap, then opened the gold chest. Sure enough, lying on top of a pile of chocolate coins, was a second friendship bracelet! This one had RACHEL embroidered on it.

"It's beautiful," Rachel exclaimed,
taking the bracelet out. "Thank you,
Florence!"

"My pleasure," Florence replied,
waving her wand and returning the girls
to human-size. The bracelet magically
tied itself around Rachel's wrist.

Suddenly, they heard footsteps
approaching. "Sounds like everyone else
is on their way — quick, out the front
door!" Florence urged.

Kirsty closed the treasure chest. She and Rachel ran in a loop around the building and back through the hall, with Florence hiding in Rachel's bag. They couldn't let anyone know that they'd found the treasure first!

They reached the front porch again just in time to hear cheers from the other kids, who were gathered by the front door. "Chocolate coins!" someone whooped. "Yum!"

Rachel had assumed that since she'd gotten her bracelet, everyone would go back to being friends, but that wasn't the case.

The kids by the door — and the goblins! — were pushing and shoving one another in order to snatch up chocolate coins, even though there were plenty to go around.

"Do you remember how I said that I added some special wishing magic to your bracelets when I made them?" Florence said quietly. "Well, now you can make your wish."

Kirsty's eyes lit up with excitement. Rachel's did, too. What should they wish for?

"Since these are friendship bracelets, maybe we should make a friendship wish?" Rachel said after a moment.

"Yes, for everyone here," Kirsty suggested.

Florence beamed. "I couldn't have said it better myself," she said.

Kirsty and Rachel held hands. "We wish that everyone could be friends again!" they said together.

Both girls felt their wrists tingle as
sparkly magic flew up into the air.
And then . . .

"Sorry I wasn't very nice to you
earlier," one boy said to another. "It's
cool that we like different sports —
it doesn't mean we can't be friends."

"I like pink *and* purple," one girl said
to the girl next to her. "But I like being
friends with you much more than any
color!"

"That's more like it," Florence said happily.

Just then, one of the adults shouted that the cookout was ready, and the kids all ran outside, laughing and joking. Only the goblins stayed behind — and they didn't look happy.

"Cheer up," Florence told them. "Here, let me make you your own friendship bracelets." She waved her wand and three bracelets appeared on the goblins' wrists. They weren't quite as magical-looking as Rachel's and Kirsty's bracelets, but the goblins looked very excited.

"And here's one to take home to Jack Frost, too," Florence said, creating a silver bracelet and handing it to the nearest goblin. "Hopefully this will help him become a good friend to others. Maybe even to the fairies!"

The goblins thanked her politely and went off, all being extra-nice to one another. "You're the ugliest goblin I've ever seen," the pirate goblin said sweetly to the wizard goblin.

"Oh, thank you!" the wizard goblin replied, blushing. "But you definitely have the pointiest nose!"

Rachel and Kirsty tried their hardest not to burst out laughing. They'd never seen the goblins being so friendly — even if their compliments were strange!

"It's been so nice to meet you," Florence said. "Thank you for all your help! I'd better return to Fairyland now. I'm sure the rest of your party will be lots of fun, now that everyone is friends again."

"Thanks, Florence," Kirsty said. "I love my bracelet — and I love being friends with the fairies!"

"Me, too," Rachel said. "See you soon, I hope."

Florence blew them a kiss and fluttered away. Once she'd gone, Kirsty and Rachel rejoined the party. Everyone was in a great mood, and there was lots of laughter and happy conversation.

"Hooray for friends," Kirsty said, slipping her arm through Rachel's.

Kirsty smiled. "And hooray for fairies, too!" she said. "I hope we have lots more adventures together!"

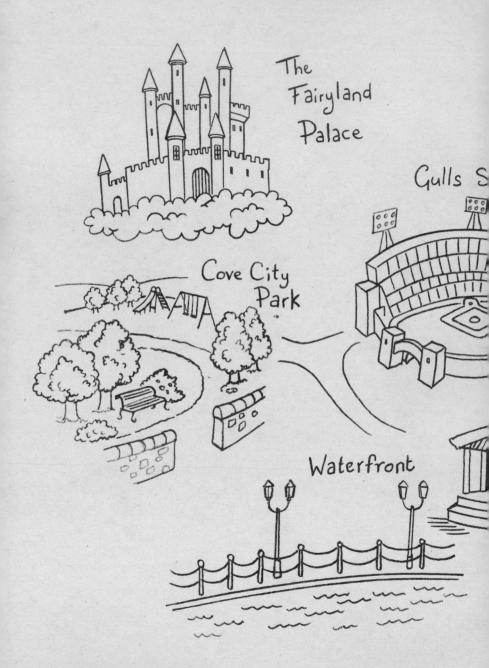

The
Fairyland
Palace

Gulls S

Cove City
Park

Waterfront

dium

Jack Frost's
Ice Castle

Cove City
Zoo

Bandshell

ZOO

I'm sick and tired of sweet celebrations
For milestones, achievements, and graduations.
I'm putting a stop to all this fun—
Thanks to me, Jack Frost, it's finally done!

The magic tulip, balloon, and diploma, too,
Are mine, pesky fairies! And there's nothing you can do.
I'll hide them away, far out of sight.
Congrats to me—now things are just right!

**Find the hidden letters in the balloons
throughout this book. Unscramble all 8 letters
to spell a special congratulations word!**

First-Pitch Fears

Contents

A Surprising Snack

"I'm so excited to go to a real professional baseball game, Kirsty!" Rachel Walker said, squeezing her best friend's hand. Together, they stepped off the city bus outside the stadium.

"Me, too!" Kirsty Tate said with a little skip. "Thanks so much for inviting me along this weekend. Cove City is the best!"

Rachel grinned. Kirsty was right—Cove City was one of her very favorite places to visit. Luckily, her cousin Ivy's family lived in the city, so Rachel and her parents came to see them often. But this weekend, they were here for a very special occasion: Ivy's high school graduation! There

were lots of activities planned, and the girls couldn't wait to see and do as much as possible during their trip. They

always had magical adventures when they were together!

Kirsty and Rachel stopped to look around inside the stadium's enormous entryway. Everything was decorated in blue and white, the colors of the Cove City Gulls baseball team. There were food carts, gift shops, trophy cases, and banners celebrating the team as far as the eye could see.

"Come on, you two!" Ivy called from up ahead, with the rest of her cousins close behind. "The field is this way!"

The girls ran to catch up to the group. "It's so cool that we get to come early to watch batting practice and meet the players," Kirsty said breathlessly.

Ivy's eyes sparkled. "I'm a huge Gulls fan," she said, "so this is the perfect way to celebrate this special weekend—here, with all of you!" She gave Rachel's and Kirsty's shoulders a squeeze.

Ivy led the group down a long hallway. As they stepped

out into the sunshine, rows of seats and the wide, green baseball field stretched out before them. Rachel and Kirsty had never seen anything like it!

"I had no idea the field was so big!" Rachel exclaimed.

Kirsty nodded in wonder. "It's hard to tell when you're watching the game on TV."

The girls followed Ivy and the rest of Rachel's cousins down to a row of blue and white seats right behind home plate.

"Settle in, everyone!" Ivy said with a big smile. "First, the team takes batting practice, and then we'll  get a chance to go onto the field."

Rachel shivered with excitement at the thought of it.

Someone dressed as Sully, the team's seagull mascot, came around to hand out popcorn, peanuts, and boxes of Cracker Jack. The group cheered wildly as the Gulls took the field. Their starting pitcher, Jim Fay, warmed up in the bullpen while other players stepped up to the plate to practice hitting.

"This is already such a great day—and it's barely even started," Rachel said to Kirsty, pulling open the top of her Cracker Jack box.

Before Kirsty could reply, the girls were hit with a rush of air and a puff of twinkling dust.

"What was that?" Kirsty cried.

Rachel looked down at her snack. "I think it came from my Cracker Jack box," she said in surprise. Then she lowered her voice, looking around to make sure none of her cousins overheard. "Kirsty, do you think that could have been . . . fairy dust?"

Kirsty's eyes grew wide. Both girls held

their breath as Rachel pulled back the flap of the box again.

Sure enough, nestled inside among the popcorn and peanuts was a tiny, sparkling fairy!

Batter Up!

"I'm so happy I found you!" the little
fairy cried. Her dark hair was pulled into
a side bun, and her purple dress stood out
inside the Cracker Jack box. The girls
had to lean in close to hear her. "I'm
Chelsea the Congratulations Fairy—and I
need your help!"

Rachel looked around to make sure

none of her cousins were
paying attention.
They were all too
busy watching
batting practice
to notice this
magical turn of
events! "It's nice
to meet you,
Chelsea," she
whispered with a smile.

"We're happy to help you," Kirsty
added, using her pinkie finger to shake
the little fairy's hand. "Let me guess—is
Jack Frost up to his old tricks again?"

Chelsea's sweet face turned sour at the
mention of Jack Frost's name. "You'd
think he'd get tired of being such a
horrible troublemaker!" she huffed.

"What did he do this time?" Rachel asked.

Chelsea sighed, sinking back onto a piece of popcorn. "He stole my three magic objects right out from under my nose! When I woke up this morning, they were missing. He must have snuck into my toadstool house while I was sleeping!" Her eyes narrowed. "If I'd been awake, there's no way he would have gotten away with it."

The girls frowned. This really was a new low for Jack Frost!

"I searched all over Fairyland, but I think he had his goblins hide the objects in your world," Chelsea continued. "I don't even know where to start looking for them!"

Kirsty popped a piece of Cracker Jack in her mouth and chewed thoughtfully. "What do your objects look like, Chelsea?"

"They're a yellow tulip, a red balloon, and a diploma," Chelsea replied. Her face fell. "Together, they help people everywhere achieve accomplishments and take important steps from one thing to the next. My tulip controls courage, helping people be brave and try new things—even if they're scary. My balloon controls confidence, helping people believe in themselves and know that they can meet their goals. And my diploma controls persistence, helping people stick with things and see them through to the end."

"Those sound really important," Rachel commented.

Chelsea flopped over dramatically. "Exactly! Without them, all sorts of accomplishments and milestones are going to turn into disasters—including graduations!"

Rachel and Kirsty both gasped. Oh, no! Ivy's graduation was tomorrow. They couldn't let it be ruined!

"Jack Frost won't get away with this!" Kirsty said, determined.

"Thank you, girls!" Chelsea cried, twirling up out of the box to give them each a peck on the cheek. She fluttered down into Kirsty's shirt pocket. "I'll stay here, out of sight, and do whatever I can to help."

Just then, Ivy clapped her hands. "Okay, everyone—batting practice is

over, which means it's our turn to go
take the field!" Her eyes glimmered as
she led the group onto the field.

"Ivy is so excited about this weekend,"
Rachel whispered to Kirsty and Chelsea.
"I don't want anything to spoil that."

As the girls stepped onto the huge field,
they looked around in awe. This was

amazing! Before they knew it, several of the Gulls players had come up to shake their hands. They split the group in half, and one side played the field while the other took turns at bat.

For a little while, Rachel and Kirsty forgot all about Chelsea's magic objects. They were having too much fun! Ivy got a huge hit, and Rachel's cousin Sam made a few incredible catches in the outfield. Rachel and Kirsty both got hits, too. But running around the bases was exhausting—*whew!*

Rachel flopped down behind home plate to take a break, and Kirsty sat next to her, cross-legged. They cheered and clapped as others stepped up to bat.

After a few minutes, Kirsty nudged Rachel. "Look at that group of bat boys over there," she said, nodding toward the dugout. "Are they supposed to be goofing around like that?"

Rachel turned her gaze to where Kirsty was looking. She was surprised she hadn't noticed the boys before, since they were making so much noise.

"Hmm," Rachel muttered. Something about the boys seemed strange. "Chelsea, have you seen these boys before?" she whispered.

Chelsea peeked out of Kirsty's pocket, and the three friends watched the bat boys shoving, poking one another with bats, and tumbling in the dirt.

Suddenly, Rachel gasped. "Kirsty, I don't think those are bat boys," she said slowly, peering at their giant feet. "They're goblins!"

The Not-So-Lucky Winner

Kirsty's eyes grew wide. "You're right!" she cried. She could see the goblins' long green noses peeking out from under their baseball caps.

"We have to keep an eye on those goblins, girls," Chelsea said urgently, biting her lip. "I'm sure they'll lead us to one of my magic objects!"

Before Rachel and Kirsty could come up with a plan, the Gulls' star pitcher, Jim Fay, whistled for everyone to join him on the pitcher's mound.

"Great job, everyone!" he said as they gathered around. "Thanks for joining us today—and a very special congratulations to Ivy on her graduation tomorrow!" He gave Ivy a high five while everyone cheered.

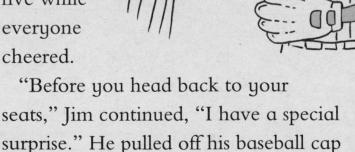

"Before you head back to your seats," Jim continued, "I have a special surprise." He pulled off his baseball cap

and held it out in front of him. "Anyone who wants to can write their name down and put it in my hat. I'll choose a name at random, and that person will get to throw the first pitch of the game today!"

The group buzzed with excitement. Rachel and Kirsty looked at each other in surprise. Wow!

Everyone wrote their names on little scraps of paper and tossed them into Jim's hat. The girls held their breath as he fished around in the hat and pulled out a name. Chelsea looked up out of Kirsty's pocket and grinned, crossing her fingers for good luck.

"And the lucky winner is . . . Kirsty!" Jim announced.

Kirsty clapped a hand over her mouth. She couldn't believe it!

The group cheered, and Rachel and Ivy both gave her a big hug. When no one was looking, Chelsea even flashed a thumbs-up and shot a burst of

sparkly, celebratory
balloons from
her wand.

"Kirsty, you
and a friend
can stay
here, near
home plate,
until game
time," Jim told
her as the rest of
the group headed up
to their seats. "I'll be back soon for
your big moment!" He winked and
headed down the tunnel toward the
locker room.

"This is so exciting!" Rachel squealed,
squeezing Kirsty's hand.

Kirsty smiled, but didn't say anything. She had been thrilled just a minute ago . . . but now she suddenly had butterflies in her stomach!

Rachel looked at her closely. "Kirsty, what's wrong?"

"I'm scared!" Kirsty admitted with a

shrug. "Thousands of people will be watching. What if I do it wrong?"

Chelsea fluttered up out of Kirsty's pocket and settled on her shoulder. She tugged Kirsty's braid gently. "I think I know what's wrong. This is all because my magic tulip is missing!" She stomped her foot. "I wish I could give Jack Frost a piece of my mind right now."

Rachel leaned over so that she was eye level with the little fairy. "Your tulip controls courage, right?" she asked.

"Exactly," Chelsea said with a nod. "Without it, Kirsty, you aren't feeling very brave at all!"

Kirsty let out a big sigh. Chelsea was right about one thing—she was feeling less brave by the minute!

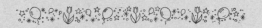

"We have to find the tulip before the game," Rachel said. She turned toward the dugout, where the rascally goblins were still goofing around, and raised an eyebrow. "Luckily, I know just where to start . . ."

Gotcha, Goblin!

Rachel, Kirsty, and Chelsea watched the goblins closely. They were climbing on top of the dugout and daring one another to jump onto the field.

"That looks dangerous," Kirsty whispered. "It's a long way down!"

Most of the goblins chickened out at the last minute and decided not to jump.

But one goblin leaped without hesitating for a second. He even did a flip in the air before landing firmly on his feet! The rest of the goblins whooped and cheered.

Chelsea drew in her breath slowly. "He's acting awfully brave . . . He must have my yellow tulip!"

The three friends peered at the brave goblin. Suddenly, Rachel nudged Kirsty and gasped.

"Look! In the buttonhole of his baseball jersey!" she said.

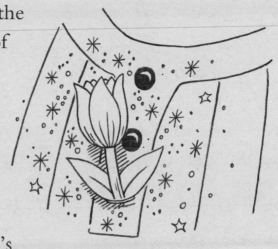

A bright yellow tulip was tucked in the goblin's buttonhole—and it was sparkling with fairy magic!

Chelsea zoomed into the air, flew a series of excited loops, and dove back into Kirsty's pocket before anyone could spot her. "That's it!" she cried in her tiny fairy voice.

Kirsty twirled her hair thoughtfully. "But how are we going to get it from him? It's right under his nose."

"I have an idea . . ." Rachel said with a grin. She leaned in to whisper the plan to her friends.

"Let's give it a try," Chelsea said, fluttering her wings anxiously inside Kirsty's pocket.

Kirsty giggled. "That tickles!"

Without a moment to waste, Rachel grabbed a baseball and Kirsty picked up a nearby bat.

"Ready?" Rachel called loudly, winding up to pitch. "Swing, batter batter batter!"

380

Kirsty swung wildly at the ball,
but missed by a mile. She sighed
dramatically. "Go again! I'll get it
this time."

But each time Rachel pitched the ball,
Kirsty swung and missed.

"Strike!" Rachel called, turn after turn.

Kirsty pretended to get frustrated.
"Ugh!" she cried, kicking the dirt next to
home plate. "I just can't seem to hit the

ball. I wish someone could show me
what I'm doing wrong . . ."

As if on cue, the goblin with the yellow
tulip dashed over from the dugout.
"You're in luck!" he bragged. "I'm an
amazing baseball player. I'll show you
how it's done!"

With that,
the goblin
took Kirsty's
bat and
hit three
pitches in a
row. He really
was a good
player! Chelsea peeked up at Kirsty from
inside her pocket, looking impressed.

"Wow," Kirsty said to the goblin.
"You're the best baseball player I've ever

met! Can you help me take a swing? I just know that I'll be able to do it if you're helping me."

The goblin smiled proudly, strutting around home plate and twirling the bat. "Of course, of course. I'm always happy to share my unbelievable talents."

Kirsty glanced down to see Chelsea roll her eyes. On the pitcher's mound, Rachel was trying to stifle a giggle. This goblin was awfully full of himself!

Kirsty made sure to stay on the goblin's good side. It was all part of the plan!

"Oh, thank you!" she said as the goblin stood behind her and helped her choke up on the bat.

"You see," the goblin began, "you just need to put your hands like this, and then when you see the ball coming, make sure you—"

But the goblin didn't have a chance to finish before Kirsty turned, plucked the magic tulip from his jersey, and quickly handed it to Chelsea. Immediately, the tulip shrunk to fairy-size! Chelsea fluttered high up into the air, out of reach, with a happy cheer.

The goblin froze, looking first at the trail of sparkling fairy dust in the air, and then down at his jersey. As he

realized what had
happened, his
mouth fell open.

"Horrible girls!
Pesky fairy!
You stole my
tulip!" he cried
indignantly,
throwing the bat
in anger.

Chelsea flew down to face
him, her hands on her hips. "Jack Frost
stole this tulip from *me*," she said firmly.
"You all really need to learn not to take
things that don't belong to you."

Before the goblin could stammer a
response, Chelsea blew each of the girls
a kiss, winked, and disappeared back to
Fairyland in the twinkling of an eye.

Magically Brave

The goblin stomped his feet and howled, "Get back here, you tricky fairy!"

But Chelsea was long gone.

From the dugout, the other goblins jeered at their friend.

"You let them take the tulip from right under your giant nose!" one cried.

"Jack Frost is going to be so mad at us!" called another.

The poor goblin looked like he didn't know what to say.

"Sorry about that," Kirsty said. "You are a great baseball player, though."

His green face lit up. "Really?" he asked hopefully.

"Absolutely," said Rachel, walking up to join them. "Maybe you could be on the Gulls one day!"

The goblin clapped his hands merrily at the thought.

Just then, the Gulls' manager called the bat boys away to get ready for the game. The goblin skipped off to join his friends.

The girls couldn't help laughing.

"Looks like it's almost game time," Rachel said, watching the stands fill with fans. "How are you feeling, Kirsty?"

Kirsty thought for a minute, then threw an arm around Rachel's shoulders. "Thanks to Chelsea and her magic tulip, I'm feeling braver than ever!"

"Are you ready, Kirsty?" Jim Fay

called, walking over. He handed her the
game ball.

"I was born ready!" Kirsty replied.

With that, Jim led her out to a spot in
front of the pitcher's mound. Kirsty
waved and laughed as the announcer
proclaimed for the whole stadium to
hear: "Throwing today's first pitch is a
very special guest of the Gulls, Miss
Kirsty Tate!"

The crowd cheered wildly. Kirsty could see Ivy and her cousins waving excitedly from their seats.

She took a deep breath, kept her eye on the catcher . . . and threw the ball right into his mitt!

More cheers rang in her ears as she and Jim jogged back to home plate together.

"You didn't seem nervous at all!"

Rachel cried, giving her a big hug.

"I wasn't," Kirsty said. "My nerves disappeared like . . . magic!"

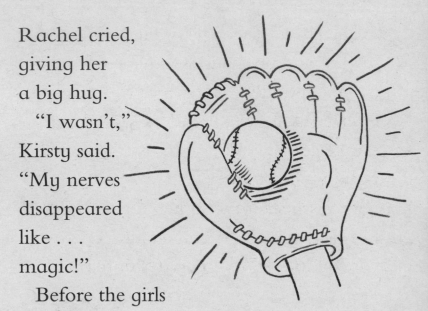

Before the girls headed up to join Ivy and the group in their seats, Jim tapped Kirsty on the shoulder. He was holding a big bouquet of flowers.

"Congratulations on a great pitch," he said, giving her a high five and handing her the flowers.

Kirsty and Rachel thanked him and wished the team good luck as they

walked off the
field.

Suddenly,
Rachel
started
giggling.
"Kirsty, did
you take a close
look at your bouquet yet?"

Kirsty shook her head and looked
down at the flowers. They were all bright
yellow tulips!

She laughed, too. "I think Chelsea
would approve!"

Much Ado at the Zoo

Contents

Animal Adventure

"I hope they have tigers!" Rachel said, linking arms with Kirsty and skipping down the city sidewalk. Cars, taxis, and buses zoomed down the busy street. Tall buildings towered all around.

Kirsty giggled. "And baboons!" She turned to smile at Rachel's parents, who strolled down the street behind the girls.

"Thanks so much for taking us to the Cove City Zoo this morning, Mr. and Mrs. Walker."

"It's nice to get out of the house and see the sights," Mrs. Walker replied.

"Besides, Ivy seemed awfully nervous about her graduation speech this afternoon," Mr. Walker added. Then he winked. "It's best that we stay out of her hair for a little while!"

Rachel raised an eyebrow at Kirsty. The girls knew that Ivy was feeling more than just regular nerves. "This is all

because two of Chelsea the Congratulations Fairy's magic objects are still missing," she whispered.

"I know," Kirsty said with a sigh. She nudged Rachel with her elbow. "But cheer up! Maybe we'll find one at the zoo. Look!"

Up ahead, the girls could see a huge iron gate topped with animal silhouettes. A colorful sign read *Welcome to the Cove City Zoo!* With a squeal, they both ran as fast as they could until they reached the gate.

"This is one of the biggest zoos in the country," Mrs. Walker said when she finally caught up.

Mr. Walker paid the admission fee and studied a map. "There's a lot to see," he said with a whistle. "You girls have your work cut out for you!"

Rachel grinned. "Can we explore on our own for a while?" she asked. Without her parents around, maybe she and Kirsty could find one of Chelsea's

magic objects . . . or maybe they'd even find Chelsea herself!

"Sure, I think that would be OK," Mrs. Walker said. "Why don't we meet in an hour by the penguin exhibit? They feed the penguins at eleven o'clock, and Ivy said we definitely shouldn't miss it." She circled it on the map.

"I love penguins!" Kirsty cried. "That sounds great."

Rachel gave
each of her
parents
a hug,
grabbed
Kirsty's hand,
and together
they ran off down the tree-lined path.

"The baboons are this way," Kirsty
said, pointing to the left.

Rachel pointed to the right. "And the

tigers are that way." Suddenly, she
stopped in her tracks. Just ahead, a
young woman in a green zookeeper
uniform sat alone on a bench. She held
her head in her hands. "Kirsty, look,"
Rachel whispered.

Kirsty peered at the woman. "She looks
awfully upset," she noted. "What do you
think could be wrong?"

"I don't know," Rachel said. "But
there's only one way to find out . . ."

Safari Magic

Rachel slowly approached the bench, with Kirsty close behind. She put a gentle hand on the zookeeper's shoulder. "Excuse me—are you OK?"

The young woman looked up in surprise. When she saw the girls' concerned faces, she gave them a small smile. "I'll be fine," she said. "Thanks for asking."

Kirsty noticed that the woman's name tag read CLARE. "You work here at the zoo, Clare?"

Clare sighed. "I'm new. Today is my first day in charge of the big penguin feeding."

"Oh!" Rachel's face lit up. "We're planning to watch that! I heard that it's a super-popular exhibit."

"It's many visitors' favorite part of the zoo," Clare said, looking even more

worried than before.
"And that makes
my problem even
worse! I've
worked with
these penguins
a lot behind the
scenes, and I
have plenty of
experience at other
zoos, too. But in our

latest practice session, everything went
wrong. The penguins wouldn't listen to
me at all!"

Rachel and Kirsty looked at each other
with raised eyebrows. Uh-oh! This must
be because of Chelsea's missing magic
objects . . .

Clare buried her head in her hands

again. "I'm sure that I'm going to disappoint all of the visitors who come to see the penguins today!"

"I wish there were something we could do to help you," Rachel said.

Kirsty squeezed Rachel's arm. "There is," she whispered. "We have to find Chelsea's magic objects—and fast!"

Rachel nodded, looking determined. "I hope everything goes better at the

feeding, Clare," she said to the
zookeeper. "We'll be cheering you on
from the audience!"

"Good luck," Kirsty added. "You'll do
great!"

Clare gave the girls a halfhearted
smile and waved as they headed down
the path.

"Poor Clare," Rachel said once they
were out of earshot.

Kirsty sighed. "This is all Jack Frost's
fault—and we're the only ones who can
help. I just wish we knew where to look!"

Together, the girls headed into the area
marked *Safari*. For a few minutes, they
completely forgot about Chelsea's magic
objects. Around every bend in the path
they spotted roaring lions, trumpeting
elephants, and towering giraffes!

"Wow!" Kirsty cried. "Those elephants were even bigger than I expected!"

"And look at that giraffe!" Rachel added, pointing. "I can barely see the top of its head behind that tall tree branch."

Kirsty squinted as the giraffe moved. "Doesn't the top of its head look a little . . . sparkly?" she asked slowly.

Rachel gasped. "It's Chelsea!"

412

Rachel was right! The tiny fairy was
perched on the giraffe's head, waving.
She fluttered down to see the girls,
leaving a trail of shimmering fairy dust
behind her. The giraffe nodded in a
friendly way and wandered off.

"Hi, girls!" Chelsea called, grinning as
she landed on Rachel's shoulder. "I was
hoping to find you here."

"We were hoping to find you, too," Kirsty said. "We've been searching for more of your magic objects, but we haven't had any luck yet."

The girls continued along the safari path, with Chelsea sitting comfortably on Rachel's shoulder.

"Things are going all wrong, Chelsea," Rachel said, looking glum. "My cousin Ivy is really nervous about her graduation speech, and we just met a zookeeper named Clare who's worried

about disappointing fans
at the penguin feeding."

Chelsea put her
hands on her hips,
suddenly looking
spunky and
determined. "This
is all because my
magic balloon is
missing!" she cried.
"It gives people
confidence. We
have to get it back!"

Something Fishy

The three friends made their way out of the safari exhibit and along another pathway, keeping their eyes open for anything magical. Colorful birds swooped overhead. A peacock even strutted right out in front of them!

Just then, Chelsea tugged on Rachel's ponytail. "One of my magic objects is nearby," she whispered excitedly. "I can sense it!"

Rachel and Kirsty peered all around, but they didn't see anything unusual. Kirsty  peeked behind a shrub along the side of the path—and jumped when a frog hopped out and landed on her foot!

"The zoo is full of magical surprises," Kirsty said, laughing. "I just hope we can find the magic we're looking for!"

The girls continued toward the tiger exhibit. As they rounded a corner in the

path, they spotted a huge cart rolling to a stop up ahead. Tied to the cart were tons and tons of balloons in all different colors!

"Wow," Rachel said. "Those are awfully pretty . . . but I thought balloons weren't allowed at the zoo."

Kirsty shook her head, suddenly looking angry. "They're not. If the animals try to eat them, they could get really hurt!"

"I wonder what all of those balloons are doing here, then," Chelsea said, narrowing her eyes suspiciously. "Something fishy is going on!"

She darted behind a nearby tree, and the girls followed. They had a perfect view of the cart from their hiding spot! They could see three workers in zoo uniforms bustling around the cart, getting ready to open for the day. One pushed the cart, the second filled balloons from a helium tank, and the third was ready to deal with customers.

"Do you notice anything strange about those workers?" Kirsty asked.

Rachel squinted. "I can't see their faces because their hats are too low," she said. Then she gasped. "But they have gigantic *green* feet!"

"Goblins!" Chelsea cried, tumbling through the air in excitement. "And they have my magic balloon with them!"

Before the girls could say anything else, they were drowned out by the goblins, arguing loudly.

Chelsea rolled her eyes and sighed. "They're fighting. What else is new?" she muttered.

The girls listened closely.

"You were supposed to keep track of it!" one goblin cried, pointing at another.

That goblin shook his head. "No, no, no! It wasn't me. I'm in charge of collecting the money."

The third goblin held up his hands. "Don't look at me!" he said. "It's not my fault you lost it!"

The first goblin threw his hat to the ground in exasperation. "Jack Frost will never forgive us!"

Rachel's eyes widened. "Did they lose your magic balloon, Chelsea?"

Chelsea winked. "No, they just can't tell which one it is—it's mixed in with all of the other balloons!"

The girls stifled their giggles. The goblins were always causing extra trouble for themselves!

"I can tell which
balloon is
mine,
though,"
Chelsea
said. "Do
you see
that
red one,
in the
middle
of the bunch on the far left side?"

Kirsty and Rachel looked closely.
"Oh, I see it now!" Kirsty whispered.
"It's shimmering with a tiny bit of
fairy magic!"

Chelsea nodded, her eyes twinkling.
Then she frowned. "But how are we
going to get it back? The goblins

may be foolish sometimes, but they
surely won't let any of the balloons out
of their sight."

"I have an idea," Kirsty said, looking
thoughtful. She leaned in to whisper the
plan to her friends, grinning. "It's crazy
enough that it just might work!"

Up in the Air

With their plan in place, Rachel and Kirsty both took a deep breath. Chelsea was safely hidden behind Rachel's ponytail as the girls walked up to the balloon cart.

"Hi!" Rachel exclaimed, waving. The goblins stopped arguing and turned to scowl at her. "We'd like to buy forty balloons, please."

The goblins stared at them in shock. The girls could almost see the dollar signs shining in their greedy eyes.

"Excuse us for just one moment, ladies," one of them said politely, holding up a bony green finger.

The three goblins huddled together, muttering frantically. They were trying to be sneaky, but Rachel and Kirsty

could still hear snippets of their
conversation.

"We need to
make sure we
don't give them
the magic
balloon! Jack
Frost would be
really angry!"

"Just think of how much money we
could make, selling forty balloons at
once. Our first sale of the day! We'll
be rich!"

Rachel looked at Kirsty, nervous.
What would the goblins decide?

Finally, three green faces turned back
toward the girls. One of the goblins
cleared his throat. "We'd be very happy
to sell you forty balloons," he said.

Kirsty breathed a sigh of relief, and Rachel squeezed her arm. The goblins hadn't been able to resist making lots of money, just as the girls had hoped!

"Oh, thank you!" Kirsty said sweetly.

One goblin began carefully collecting forty balloons from the cart. He winced with the addition of each new balloon to the bunch. He was obviously worried about handing over the magic balloon by accident!

A tiny voice made Rachel's smile even wider. "My magic balloon is in the bunch now!" Chelsea whispered, tugging gently on Rachel's ponytail.

Rachel gave Kirsty a wink.

The goblin untied a few more balloons to add to the gigantic bunch in his hand. Suddenly . . . he was lifted up into the air! He was holding so many balloons that they carried him right up off the ground!

"HELP!" the goblin shrieked, kicking and flailing in midair. He clung to the balloon strings for dear life. "Help me!"

His goblin friends stared up at him in shock, frozen. By the time they made a move, the goblin with the balloons had floated too high. They couldn't reach him!

Just then, Chelsea sprang into action. She fluttered out from behind Rachel's ponytail and twirled up into the air, her party skirt floating around her.

"I'll make a deal with you!" she said cheerfully, hovering next to the panicking goblin.

His eyes were squeezed shut in fear, but they popped open when he heard Chelsea's voice. "Fairies!" he cried. "I should have known you pesky fairies were behind this trick!"

Chelsea put her hands on her hips and narrowed her eyes. "Would you like my help or not?"

The goblin looked down at the ground, which was getting farther and farther

away. "OK, OK!" he squealed. "What do you want?"

"It's simple," Chelsea said with a casual shrug. "You're holding my magic balloon. Just hand it over, and I'll get you down from there."

The goblin scowled. Below, his friends protested, jumping up and down and shaking their heads.

"Don't do it!" one cried.

"Jack Frost will be furious!" the other added with a shudder.

"Don't you think I know that?!"
squealed the goblin in the air.

Kirsty looked at Rachel and crossed
her fingers. They were so close to getting
Chelsea's magic balloon back—but what
if the goblin said no?

Balloon Bust

Chelsea zoomed around the goblin and the balloons, flying in a few dizzying loops. "Do we have a deal?" she asked.

The goblin glanced down at her—and squealed again when he saw how high he'd floated! "All right!" he cried. "Take whatever you want!"

On the ground below, Rachel and

Kirsty whooped
and gave
each other
a high five.
Chelsea
didn't waste
a moment.
In the blink
of an eye, she

flew up, plucked her magic balloon out
of the bunch, and shrunk it down to
fairy-size. She held tight to it with one
hand while carefully using her wand to
make a few of the goblin's other balloons
disappear. As each balloon vanished, the
goblin slowly lowered to the ground.
When he landed on the pavement, he
shouted with joy.

His friends weren't so happy, though.

"This is all your fault!" one hollered.

The other chimed in, "You ruined everything!"

Rachel couldn't listen to them bicker any longer. "You shouldn't have balloons at the zoo anyway," she said. "They're dangerous for the animals!"

The goblins looked sheepish. For once, they had nothing to say!

Chelsea swooped out of the sky and

flicked her wand. Fairy dust glimmered in the air. When it cleared, all of the goblins' balloons had vanished.

The goblins grumbled under their breaths and turned back to their empty cart. Together, they pushed it down the path. The girls could hear them muttering, "Pesky fairies ruin everything!" as they disappeared around a bend.

Chelsea gave Rachel and Kirsty each a kiss on the cheek. "I couldn't have done it without you, girls!" She tugged on the string of her magic balloon. "Now I need to get this back to Fairyland, so people everywhere can feel confident about trying new things."

Kirsty looked at her watch. "It's almost eleven o'clock already—time for the penguin feeding! I hope your balloon can help Clare with the penguins."

Chelsea winked. "You'd better hurry up. I think today's penguin feeding is going to be something you won't want to miss!"

And with that, she vanished in a swirl of sparkles.

Rachel grabbed Kirsty's hand. The two friends ran along the wooded pathways

until they came
to the penguin
exhibit. Mr.
and Mrs.
Walker waved
to them from a
spot in the
stands, and the
girls scurried
up the steps to
join them.

"You're just in time!"
Mrs. Walker said with a smile. "Did you
have fun exploring the zoo?"

"It was an adventure!" Rachel said.

Mr. Walker handed over two red
slushies in silly penguin cups. "We
thought you might be thirsty."

The girls' eyes lit up. They thanked

him and sipped their icy drinks as the announcer came over the loudspeaker.

"Ladies and gentlemen, boys and girls—welcome to Cove City Zoo's famous penguin feeding!"

The crowd cheered, but Rachel and Kirsty couldn't help feeling nervous as Clare stepped out onto a rock next to the water. She waved to the audience,

and the girls waved back, giving her
thumbs-up. When Clare spotted them,
her face lit up with a huge grin.

"She doesn't look worried anymore,"
Kirsty whispered.

Rachel chewed on her straw. "I hope
the return of Chelsea's balloon has given
Clare some confidence!"

As the feeding began, it was clear that
Clare and the penguins were a perfect

team! The penguins performed every trick that Clare asked, happily gobbling up the fish that she offered them. The penguins splashed in the water, spun on the rocks, and made everyone laugh.

Rachel sighed in relief. "I think we found Chelsea's balloon just in time," she said. "Hopefully Ivy is feeling better about her graduation speech, too."

Kirsty cheered as one of the penguins slid across a rock on his belly. "I bet she is," she said. "And I bet her speech is going to be perfectly magical!"

Graduation
Celebration

Contents

Graduation Gone Bad

"What a beautiful spot for a graduation!" Kirsty said as she and Rachel walked into Cove City Park. The park was filled with leafy green trees, colorful flower beds, and sparkling fountains.

Rachel grinned. "It's hard to believe we're right in the middle of a city, isn't it?"

Up ahead,
Mr. and Mrs.
Walker walked
alongside
Ivy and her
parents.
"Come on,
girls!" Mr.
Walker called,
pointing to an
enormous lawn. "The
ceremony is this way!"

Rachel and Kirsty raced to catch up,
and they both gasped in awe as the lawn
spread out before them. Rows of white
folding chairs faced a huge stage. Just
beyond the stage was the glimmering
cove, which twinkled beautifully in the
afternoon sunlight.

"Ivy, this place looks perfect," Rachel said softly, squeezing her cousin's arm. "I'm so excited for your big day!"

Ivy smiled, straightening her cap and smoothing the wrinkles out of her long, black graduation gown. "Thanks! I have to go do a sound check so I know how to use the microphone when it's time for my speech. Wish me luck!"

The whole
family hugged
Ivy and
waved as she
headed to
the stage.

"Well,
girls," Mrs.
Walker said,
turning to Rachel
and Kirsty, "the
ceremony doesn't start for a while yet.
The rest of the family will be here later.
Do you two want to explore in the
meantime? We'll save some seats."

"That sounds great!" Kirsty said. Once
the adults had walked away, she turned
to Rachel. "Do you want to check out
the cove? It looks awfully magical . . ."

Rachel winked. "I sure hope it is!"

As the girls headed past the stage to the waterfront, they couldn't help noticing all sorts of commotion backstage. People seemed to be running around frantically.

A loud squeak rang through the air. "The speakers aren't working right!" someone cried.

"That's nothing," another voice chimed in. "We just found out that

Principal Doogan is stuck in traffic—and he has all of the diplomas in his car!"

Someone else piped up. "Has anyone seen the master list of graduates' names? It was right here, but now I can't find it anywhere!"

Rachel and Kirsty looked at each other in dismay. They knew exactly why everything was going wrong—and they were the only ones who could fix it!

"We have to find Chelsea's missing magic diploma," Rachel whispered urgently. "I don't even know

where to start
looking, though."

Kirsty sighed.
"Queen Titania
always says we
should let the
magic find
us . . . but we
don't have much
time. If we don't track
down the diploma soon, Ivy's graduation
ceremony will be an absolute disaster!"

Diploma Dilemma

Rachel and Kirsty left the chaotic stage behind and headed to the waterfront. The cove sparkled in the sunshine. It was so big that the girls could barely see where it opened up into the ocean!

"Look at all the boats out there," Rachel said, pointing at sailboats,

rowboats, kayaks, and motorboats
bobbing on the calm water.

Kirsty nodded. "And
so many people
are flying kites
on the beach!"
The colorful
kites sailed
overhead,
their tails
blowing in the
breeze. There
were kites in every
color of the rainbow!

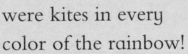

As both girls peered up, Rachel
suddenly squeezed Kirsty's arm. "Did you
see that?"

"That kite is glimmering a little bit!"
Kirsty said excitedly, noticing a beautiful

purple kite with multicolored bows on its tail. She turned to Rachel, her eyes shining. "Do you think it could be . . . ?"

Just then, the kite dipped closer to the ground. The girls squinted to get a better look. Sure enough, they could see a tiny figure perched on the kite, her dark bangs blowing in the breeze.

"It's Chelsea!" Rachel cried.

Chelsea darted through the air so quickly that no one else was able to spot her. Rachel and Kirsty could hear her

laugh as she fluttered down and landed
lightly on Kirsty's shoulder.

"Hi, girls!" the little fairy called out
cheerfully, grinning up at them. "I'm so
happy to see you again."

"We're
happy
to see
you, too,
Chelsea,"
Kirsty
said, and
Rachel
used her
pinkie finger to give Chelsea a tiny
high five.

The girls made their way to a grassy
hill near the water, away from the
crowds. "I think we can talk here

462

without anyone seeing us," Rachel noted. She plucked a fluffy dandelion from the grass, and blew the seeds into the air.

"Everyone in Fairyland was thrilled to see my magic balloon," Chelsea reported. "I can't thank you enough for your help tracking it down!"

Kirsty frowned. "Things are still all mixed-up here, I'm afraid," she said.

"Ivy's graduation starts soon, and nothing seems to be going right!" She blew on a dandelion with a frustrated huff.

Chelsea put her hands on her hips, looking determined. "We have to figure out what those terrible goblins have done with my magic diploma! Where should we start?"

Rachel and Kirsty both shrugged.

"I don't have a clue," Rachel said, staring down at her hands.

Kirsty nodded and lay back in the grass with a sigh. "Yeah, why bother? We'll never find your diploma in time to fix Ivy's graduation, anyway."

Chelsea
furrowed her
tiny eyebrows
and looked
at the girls
carefully.
Suddenly,
she snapped
her fingers.
"This is all
because of
my missing
diploma!" she
exclaimed. "It helps people be
persistent and see tasks through to
the end. Without it, you're both thinking
of giving up." She tugged on Kirsty's
braid with a twinkle in her eye. "But

that's why I need your help more than ever!"

Rachel and Kirsty both sat up straight, as though they'd been shocked out of their stupor. Chelsea was right!

Eye on the Prize

Before either Rachel or Kirsty could say anything, some noise out on the water caught their attention.

"What's going on out there?" Chelsea murmured, hovering above Rachel's head to get a better look.

The three friends could see a big green boat bobbing in the cove. A group of boys was yelling and laughing as they did cannonballs off the side of the boat into the water. Every time one of them landed, they splashed people in kayaks and canoes all around.

"How rude!" Kirsty said indignantly.

Rachel shook her head. "Why would anyone act like that?"

At that, Chelsea gasped and did an

excited tumble in
the air. "Not
why, WHO!"
she said with
a wink.

"Goblins!"
Rachel and
Kirsty cried
together, their
faces lighting up.

The boat was too far away to see if the
boys really were goblins or not, but as
the girls looked more closely, they noticed
a huge flag fluttering off the stern of the
boat. It was green . . . and had a picture
of a giant, sneering goblin face on it!

Kirsty pointed out the flag to Chelsea.
"That boat out there definitely belongs to
the goblins!"

"I'll bet they have my magic diploma," Chelsea said with a grin. "It's so close, I can feel it!"

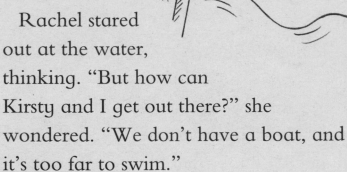

Rachel stared out at the water, thinking. "But how can Kirsty and I get out there?" she wondered. "We don't have a boat, and it's too far to swim."

The friends were silent for a moment. Then Chelsea clapped her hands in delight. "I have the perfect solution—I'll turn you both into fairies! Then we can all fly out to the boat together."

"Ooh, I love being a fairy!" Rachel said with a happy sigh.

"Me, too," Kirsty added. "Let's do it!"

With no time to waste, Chelsea murmured a spell under her breath and waved her wand. A shower of purple sparkles rained down on the girls. Before they knew it, they were the same size as Chelsea—and they had lovely, shimmery wings on their backs!

Kirsty fluttered her wings and smiled as she rose into the air. "This is the best feeling in the world," she said. "Come on, let's go!"

Rachel and Chelsea zipped up behind her as Kirsty darted out across the water. In no time at all, they reached the goblins' boat. Silently, they landed near the stern of the boat and hid behind the flapping goblin flag.

Luckily, the goblins were too busy causing chaos to notice them! But before long,

the green troublemakers climbed out
of the water and lounged
lazily in the sun.

One big-nosed
goblin yawned.
"This is the
life!" He sighed
contentedly.
"We should do
this more often."

A goblin in a
baseball cap
nodded in agreement.
"Here, it's just us. We don't have to
worry about anyone stealing the magic
diploma. We can just relax all day and
enjoy ourselves!"

Rachel, Kirsty, and Chelsea all looked
at one another and smiled. Not only did

the goblins definitely have Chelsea's
magic diploma—but they were also
about to get some surprise visitors!

But where was the diploma? Was it in
a goblin's pocket? Hidden down below
the boat deck? It could be anywhere!
The fairies scanned the deck frantically,
looking for a telltale sparkle.

Suddenly, Kirsty giggled. "Look!" she
whispered, pointing to a goblin leaning

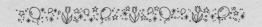

over the side of the boat. He was peering
out to sea through a telescope.

"Wait a minute," Rachel said,
catching on. "That's not a telescope at
all . . . he's looking through your magic
diploma, Chelsea!"

Diploma
Dodge

Rachel, Kirsty, and Chelsea watched the
goblin carefully. Whispering, they came
up with a plan to get the diploma back.
It was risky, but they had to try!

The three friends took to the air and
silently fluttered down near the goblin,
who was still peering at the horizon
through the diploma. On Chelsea's sign,

all three fairies suddenly began to fly faster and faster! They zipped around the goblin's head, wings buzzing.

"*Argh!*" the goblin cried frantically, swatting them away. "I hate bugs! Shoo! Shoo!"

Their plan was working—the goblin thought they were bees or flies. They were moving so fast, he had no idea that he was surrounded by fairies!

There was no time to celebrate, though. Rachel, Kirsty, and Chelsea had to keep ducking, dodging, and swooping as the goblin flapped his hands and tried to knock them away.

Kirsty dipped under the goblin's flailing hand just in time, zooming up around his big ears. *Whew!*

Seconds later, Chelsea almost crashed into the goblin's nose when he unexpectedly turned his head! At the last minute, she did a spectacular tumble in the air, up and over his nose. That was close!

"Whoa!" Rachel cried as the goblin made contact with one of her wings and sent her spiraling out over the side of the boat. For a second, she was totally out of control! Was she going to crash right into the water?

Flapping her wings as hard as she could, Rachel righted herself and sailed upward. Not a moment too soon, her toes skimmed the surface of the water as she zoomed into the sky. If she hadn't regained control, her wings would have gotten wet, and she wouldn't have been able to fly at all! Rachel took a deep breath and rejoined her friends.

The goblin continued to dance around and swat the air. Nearby, his friends watched from their lounge chairs, laughing at him.

"Are you scared of a little bee?" one called out.

Another chuckled. "It looks like you're no match for those tiny bugs!"

The goblin flailed wildly, getting more and more frustrated. Finally, he swatted the air so hard that he flung the magic diploma right out of his hand. It went flying overboard!

"Oh, no! It's going to land in the water!" Kirsty cried.

Chelsea darted through the air like a streak of light. "Not if I can help it!" She used her powerful wings to swoop down and scoop up the diploma just before it splashed into the water. As her little hand touched it, the diploma shrank to fairy-size. It was safe at last!

Once Chelsea had the diploma, Rachel and Kirsty pulled up short and hovered above the goblin's head, breathing heavily. They were exhausted!

The goblin's eyes widened when he realized what had happened. He groaned and shook his fist at the girls. "You pesky fairies again!"

The other goblins weren't laughing anymore. In fact, they looked angry! They joined their friend at the railing, peering up at Rachel, Kirsty, and Chelsea.

"Why can't you just leave us alone?" one whined.

Another goblin stomped in frustration. "You're always getting us in trouble with Jack Frost!"

Rachel looked at them pointedly. "YOU'RE always taking things that don't belong to you. That's not right!"

The goblins all looked down and scuffed their big feet. They were silent for a moment, before one mumbled, "Jack Frost is mad at us, anyway. This is just going to make it worse."

Kirsty couldn't help feeling a little sorry for the goblins. "Why is he angry with you?" she asked, perching on the railing.

"He just graduated from his master class in Ice Magic," explained the goblin who'd dropped the diploma. "We all kind of forgot to congratulate him."

Another goblin looked sad. "We didn't mean to! But he decided that if he wasn't going to be congratulated for a job well done, no one would. That's why he stole your magic objects," he finished, looking at Chelsea and her little diploma with a shrug.

Chelsea crossed her arms. "Well, I can't give you the diploma back," she said. "It's not fair for Jack Frost to ruin everyone's special days."

"But maybe we can help you cheer him up!" Rachel said suddenly. She grinned. "Why don't you throw Jack Frost a surprise party at his Ice Castle?"

Kirsty smiled at her best friend. "That's a great idea, Rachel! I bet he'll be so thrilled about the party that he won't even be mad that you lost the magic diploma," she told the goblins.

The goblins began to dance around the boat deck. "I have to admit, you little fairies have some really big ideas!" one of them exclaimed.

"We just have to decide on a theme," the big-nosed goblin said. "How about an icy luau?"

The goblin in the baseball cap rolled his eyes. "That's a terrible idea! It should clearly be a frosty pirate-themed party."

The rest of the
goblins all groaned
and began yelling
at once.

Chelsea put
an arm around
each of the girls
and giggled.
"Typical!" she said.
"Come on, let's get
back to the park."

With Chelsea in the lead, the
three friends darted over the
glittering water, leaving the boat full of
squabbling goblins behind.

A Frosty Finish

The fairy friends reached the shore and flitted down to land behind a tree, out of sight. There, Chelsea gave Rachel and Kirsty each a big hug. Then she turned them back to their normal size with a quick flick of her wand.

"Congratulations, girls!" Chelsea cried, hovering in the air before them and

squeezing her
diploma to
her chest. "You
did it! I can't
thank you
enough for all
your help."
With a wave, she
disappeared in a
swirl of glittery fairy magic.

Rachel put an arm around Kirsty's
shoulders. "Another magical mission
complete!" she declared.

But before Kirsty could reply, a big
gust of chilly wind blew in from the cove.
Both girls shivered! They watched as
boats teetered precariously on the water,
kites broke from their strings, and the
grass took on an icy sheen.

"I don't like the looks of this," Kirsty said through chattering teeth.

A bolt of lightning crashed out of the sky and landed in a stand of trees nearby, making everyone on the beach scatter in fear. Rachel and Kirsty ducked behind a bench, but they knew that it wasn't real lightning. It was a bolt of ice lightning—and it was carrying Jack Frost!

"Come on," Rachel said, heading for the trees. "We need to get Jack Frost back to Fairyland before he ruins Ivy's graduation—or worse, before anyone spots him!"

The girls sprinted past the trees . . . and came face-to-face with Jack Frost. They'd met him many times before, of course, but his icy sneer was always shocking!

"What are you doing here?" Kirsty demanded, crossing her arms.

Jack Frost whirled to face her, scowling. "None of your business! I don't have to tell you pesky girls anything."

Rachel stepped forward. "We heard that you graduated from your master class in Ice Magic," she said gently. "That's really impressive!"

"Yeah, well, you're the only one who thinks so," Jack Frost huffed, his face softening a little. "No one even bothered to

congratulate me. So even though that
horrible fairy tricked my goblins into
giving back her magic object, I'm here
to make sure that this graduation is
ruined!" He frowned.

"If you want
something
done right, I
guess you just
have to do it
yourself."

Kirsty and
Rachel
exchanged
glances.

"You know," Kirsty said carefully, "the
goblins were just telling us that they were
awfully proud of you." She lowered her
voice to a whisper. "We're not supposed

to say anything, but I think they were hoping to celebrate with you at the Ice Castle later today."

Jack Frost's eyes grew very wide. "Celebrate? Like a . . . party?" he said slowly.

"I think they wanted you to be really surprised, which is why they waited to throw the party until today," Rachel explained carefully.

A huge smile covered Jack Frost's icy face. He threw his hands in the air. "Of course! That makes perfect sense! I should have known! After all, it takes a while to plan a big, important bash."

Kirsty glanced down at her watch. "Exactly! I just hope you don't miss it . . ."

Jack Frost gasped. "They can't start without the guest of honor! I have to

go!" He disappeared in a burst of chilly
air and swirling snowflakes.

Rachel flopped down on the ground.
"That was close!"

"You're telling me," Kirsty said with a
relieved sigh. "Now we need to get
back—Ivy's graduation is about to start!"

Rachel jumped to her feet, and
together the girls ran to the main lawn

of the park. They quickly found Rachel's parents and took their seats just as music began to play. To their relief, everything seemed to be in place! The speakers were working, Principal Doogan had arrived with the diplomas, and the list of the graduates' names was up on the podium where it belonged.

The girls caught their breath as they watched the graduates file down the

aisle, wearing caps and gowns. When Ivy walked by, she waved and gave her family a huge smile. Rachel and Kirsty couldn't help cheering!

"I can't wait to hear Ivy's big speech and see her collect her diploma," Rachel whispered.

Kirsty squeezed her best friend's hand. "We know she's going to do great, thanks to Chelsea!"

SPECIAL EDITION

Don't miss any of Rachel and Kirsty's
other fairy adventures!

Check out this magical
sneak peek of

Skyler
the Fireworks Fairy!

BOOM! BOOM! BOOM!

"Rachel, what is it?" Kirsty asked as the two girls raced across the lawn.

"I'm not sure," Rachel admitted when they finally came to a stop. "But something told me we just had to get outside and into the garden." Rachel tried to catch her breath. "I just couldn't sit there anymore."

"I understand. I started to feel the same way," Kirsty shared. "It was like I could hear tiny explosions in my head all through lunch. Is that what you were talking about when we first got here?"

"Do they start with a soft fizzing sound and then get louder?" Rachel asked.

Kirsty nodded.

"I think we're both hearing the same thing! I'm glad it's not just in my head," Rachel said. "I think they're coming from over there," Rachel motioned to a large collection of garden gnomes that decorated the south end of the yard.

"Oh, they're so funny," Kirsty said, admiring their brightly colored hats

and round faces. "Gran has so many
gnomes now!"

The two friends hurried toward the
garden gnomes. "The fizzing is getting
louder," Rachel said.

The tallest gnome had a lopsided grin
and polka-dotted suspenders. Kirsty
noticed a faint stream of sparkles
beginning to shoot up from his pointy
red hat.

Kirsty looked at her friend. Rachel gave her an encouraging smile. Kirsty reached out. Just as her hand brushed against the garden gnome, a series of tiny, sparkling fireworks erupted into the air. *BOOM! BOOM! BOOM!*

As soon as the fireworks dissipated, a small fairy appeared, her glittery wings lifting her into the air. The wand she held was spouting rainbow sparkles that lit up like fireworks. The fairy looked sporty and fun in red capri pants, and a purple-and-white striped shirt. Her light-brown skin practically glowed, and her wavy brown hair cascaded past her shoulders.

"Hooray! You're here!" the fairy cheered. "I was getting worried, waiting so long, but all my friends back in Fairyland said I could count on you. It's my pleasure to finally meet you, Kirsty and Rachel. My name is Skyler the Fireworks Fairy."

The girls took turns introducing themselves. Finally, Kirsty asked the question that was on both their minds. "Skyler, what are you doing here in Honeydown?" she wondered.

Kirsty and Rachel exchanged looks of concern. "Is Jack Frost up to his old tricks again?" The girls could hardly count the times they'd had to go up against him and his troublemaking goblins.

"You guessed it!" Skyler announced, pointing her wand at Kirsty. "It all started when he complained about being tired and bored. One of his goblins

suggested that he might need a vacation. Jack Frost really liked the idea." Skyler put her hands on her hips, and a scowl replaced the smile on her face. "Now, there's nothing wrong with taking vacations, but there's nothing right about what Jack Frost and the goblins did next. Here, you can see for yourself. My magic bubble will replay the important scenes for us."

Skyler lifted her wand, and out burst a pale blue firework that grew to the size of a large puddle. When the sparkles faded, a clear bubble was in its place. Inside the bubble was a picture. Kirsty and Rachel recognized the location at once. They were staring at the inside of Jack Frost's Ice Castle! Jack Frost was listening closely to one of the goblins.

"I miss the vacations I took when I was little," the goblin pouted, his green face mopey. "We'd go to small towns, and there would be candy and gift shops, funny parades in the town square, and a lot of time to just run around and be silly."

The girls watched the bubble. Inside, Jack Frost nodded his head as the goblin continued. Just then, another goblin spoke up. "Yes! I love how they'd have all kinds of little traditions that made everything seem fun. Like bird-watching every Saturday morning and eating toasted bogmallows right after!"

Rachel and Kirsty looked at each other uncertainly. The girls couldn't picture a noisy goblin going bird-watching. They'd scare away all the birds! But the other goblins soon started to get excited, too. "Yes! We need reminders of all the fun stuff. Parades! Decorations! Sweet treats! The stuff that makes little celebrations feel festive!"

"That's it!" Jack Frost exclaimed. "I want to go to a place that lets me

feel like a kid
again!"

"That's funny,"
Kirsty said.
"That's exactly
how my grandparents
describe Honeydown."

"Exactly," Skyler said, hovering over
the girls' shoulders. "That's why they are
all here. It sounds fine, right? Almost
sweet, but then they had to be selfish
and ruin it." The picture in the magic
bubble quickly changed. Now it showed
a cozy toadstool cottage with a red
polka-dotted roof. "That's my house,"
Skyler explained. "And those goblins
were not invited."

Rachel and Kirsty gasped as they
watched what happened next. The goblins

snuck into the house and stole three items, one by one. "Jack Frost sent them after my three magic objects, because he wanted to make sure he would have the most perfect vacation getaway ever. As the Fireworks Fairy, it's my job to protect life's little traditions. I'm in charge of all those things that the goblins were just talking about!" Skyler's tiny hands closed into fists and she shook them. "But my magic doesn't really work if I don't have the objects. I can't help make things festive and fun, and I can't keep things from going horribly wrong."

All at once, the bubble picture popped.

"Oh, great!" Skyler complained. "Now that's not working, either."

"Don't worry." Rachel quickly comforted the fairy. "I think we got the idea. The goblins are trying to create a cozy, fun vacation for Jack Frost, so they stole your magic objects."

"Yes," Skyler said with a sigh. "And when I tried to stop them, Jack Frost suddenly appeared and created a whirlwind of icy magic. That wind picked up all the goblins and sent them into the human world, so it would be harder for me to find them."

"You think the goblins are here? In Honeydown?" Kirsty asked, looking around nervously.

"Yes, and they have my objects.

Will you help me find them?" Skyler
asked.

Kirsty and Rachel agreed at once. It
sounded like they had another fairy
mission!

"Why do they need the magic
objects?" Rachel wondered. "Why can't
Jack Frost just go on vacation without
bothering anyone else?"

"That's a good question," Skyler said.
"I'm not sure what he has planned. But
I do know that until we get my objects
back, the fun traditions of vacation will
be ruined for everyone!"

The Missing Magic

"OK," Skyler began. Her tone had suddenly turned very businesslike. "As you know, there isn't much time. This whole week is jam-packed with fun events in Honeydown. As long as the goblins have my objects, anything could go wrong." The fairy paced in midair, her wings fluttering in time to an imaginary military march.

Kirsty and Rachel listened closely as Skyler filled them in on the details of their task.

"First, we need to find my magic cupcake," Skyler explained. "You know how you need to follow a recipe to make a great cake?" The girls nodded. "You also need to have a plan for traditions. Without thinking things through, they won't turn out they way you want them, and then no one will be happy."

"That makes sense," Kirsty said. "We'll try to find that first."

"What are the other magic objects?" Rachel asked. "Just so we'll be prepared."

"The second is a string of bunting," answered Skyler.

"Bunting? What's that?" Kirsty wondered.

"You've seen bunting before," Skyler assured her. "Bunting is all those strings of cute, colorful triangles hanging around town. Bunting is often used at the opening of a new store, or a used-car lot."

"Oh, I love that!" Kirsty responded. "It looks so happy. I just never knew its name before."

"And the last object is my magic sparkler," Skyler said. "You'll be able to tell it's mine because it never goes out."

Both girls nodded, feeling relieved that they had a plan for rescuing everyone's fun-filled vacation celebrations.

"Now, if you don't mind," Skyler said, "I'd like to focus on our first object. There's still a lot of planning necessary for Honeydown's birthday bash, so I want to get the magic cupcake back to Fairyland safe and sound."

"You can count on us," Rachel said confidently.

Just then, the door to the grass-roofed cottage opened. Kirsty's grandparents and parents came out. "I don't understand why you would make the cake without a recipe. That's just silly," Gran said in a playful, but scolding tone. "If it's an old family recipe, you need to follow the recipe."

Gramps didn't respond. He just shuffled around looking grumpy.

"Uh-oh," Skyler said. "It looks like the troubles are already starting."

"And it looks like my parents are leaving," Kirsty pointed out.

"Quick, Skyler, you can hide in my pocket," Rachel offered, tugging on the loose fabric of her shirt so the fairy could slip right in.

The girls hurried over and gave the
Tates big hugs.

"I can't believe we won't
see you until the weekend,"
Mrs. Tate said, kissing
Kirsty on the head.
"I'm sure you'll find
a way to keep busy,"
Mr. Tate added.
"I'm sure we will,"
Kirsty said with a giggle
as she snuck a glance at
the little lump in Rachel's shirt pocket.

As soon as Kirsty's parents had driven
off, Gramps pulled out his own car keys.
"Well, since my cake ended up tasting
like stale toothpaste and cough syrup,
I'm going into town. I'm still hungry,
and they have the cupcake social today."

RAINBOW magic™

Which Magical Fairies Have You Met?

- ❏ The Rainbow Fairies
- ❏ The Weather Fairies
- ❏ The Jewel Fairies
- ❏ The Pet Fairies
- ❏ The Dance Fairies
- ❏ The Music Fairies
- ❏ The Sports Fairies
- ❏ The Party Fairies
- ❏ The Ocean Fairies
- ❏ The Night Fairies
- ❏ The Magical Animal Fairies
- ❏ The Princess Fairies
- ❏ The Superstar Fairies
- ❏ The Fashion Fairies
- ❏ The Sugar & Spice Fairies
- ❏ The Earth Fairies
- ❏ The Magical Crafts Fairies
- ❏ The Baby Animal Rescue Fairies
- ❏ The Fairy Tale Fairies

■ SCHOLASTIC

Find all of your favorite fairy friends at
scholastic.com/rainbowmagic

SCHOLASTIC and associated
logos are trademarks and/or
registered trademarks of Scholastic Inc.
© 2015 Rainbow Magic Limited.
HIT and the HIT Entertainment logo are
trademarks of HIT Entertainment Limited.

RMFAIRY13

SPECIAL EDITION

Which Magical Fairies Have You Met?

- ❑ Joy the Summer Vacation Fairy
- ❑ Holly the Christmas Fairy
- ❑ Kylie the Carnival Fairy
- ❑ Stella the Star Fairy
- ❑ Shannon the Ocean Fairy
- ❑ Trixie the Halloween Fairy
- ❑ Gabriella the Snow Kingdom Fairy
- ❑ Juliet the Valentine Fairy
- ❑ Mia the Bridesmaid Fairy
- ❑ Flora the Dress-Up Fairy
- ❑ Paige the Christmas Play Fairy
- ❑ Emma the Easter Fairy
- ❑ Cara the Camp Fairy
- ❑ Destiny the Rock Star Fairy
- ❑ Belle the Birthday Fairy

- ❑ Olympia the Games Fairy
- ❑ Selena the Sleepover Fairy
- ❑ Cheryl the Christmas Tree Fairy
- ❑ Florence the Friendship Fairy
- ❑ Lindsay the Luck Fairy
- ❑ Brianna the Tooth Fairy
- ❑ Autumn the Falling Leaves Fairy
- ❑ Keira the Movie Star Fairy
- ❑ Addison the April Fool's Day Fairy
- ❑ Bailey the Babysitter Fairy
- ❑ Natalie the Christmas Stocking Fairy
- ❑ Lila and Myla the Twins Fairies
- ❑ Chelsea the Congratulations Fairy
- ❑ Carly the School Fairy
- ❑ Angelica the Angel Fairy
- ❑ Blossom the Flower Girl Fairy

3 stories in each one!

SCHOLASTIC and associated logos are trademarks and/or registered trademarks of Scholastic Inc.
© 2015 Rainbow Magic Limited.
HIT and the HIT Entertainment logo are trademarks of HIT Entertainment Limited.

📖 SCHOLASTIC

Find all of your favorite fairy friends at
scholastic.com/rainbowmagic

HiT entertainment

RMSPECIAL17

RAINBOW magic ™

Magical fun for everyone!
Learn fairy secrets, send
friendship notes, and more!

SCHOLASTIC and associated
logos are trademarks and/or
registered trademarks of Scholastic Inc.
© 2015 Rainbow Magic Limited.
HIT and the HIT Entertainment logo
are trademarks of HIT Entertainment
Limited.

■SCHOLASTIC

HiT entertainment

www.scholastic.com/rainbowmagic

RMACTIV4